THE BAKLAVA WITCH

BROOMSTICK BAKERY #4

LAURA GREENWOOD

BLURB

When Clover decided to publish a recipe book based on the cakes they make at Broomstick Bakery, the last thing she expected was to find romance.

Tyler didn't think he'd fall for the gorgeous witch who walked into his office, but the more he gets to know her, the more he realises that this could be something special.

With the launch of Clover's cookbook drawing closer, can the two of them figure out what's between them?

-

The Baklava Witch is a paranormal romance and part of the Broomstick Bakery series. It includes witchy bakers, a workplace romance, and a standalone m/f romance.

ONE

CLOVER

THE SCENT of freshly baking cake fills the air as I approach the bakery. I don't know whether it's just a general bake, or if Oakley has a wedding order on, but it smells divine. Which is good news for us, it'll mean that we get more sales from the people who live around here tomorrow. It always happens when something tasty is being cooked.

I slip through the side door and head to the seating area where my siblings are all waiting for me.

"Hey." I sit in the seat next to Ash and grab my mug from the middle of the table, glad that one of my sisters knows me well enough to make my coffee in advance. Though if I'd thought about it, I might have grabbed everyone's coffee order from Willow's shop before coming here.

"You're late, Clover," Rowen says somewhat sternly, though it's nothing compared to how she was before she started dating Edward. Love has really mellowed her out, not that she'll admit it.

"Sorry, I got held up on a call," I admit.

"A call about what?" Hazel eyes me suspiciously.

"You know I said that a company was interested in my cookbook?"

Rowen nods.

"They asked me to come in to meet my editor to set up the release date and check out a few of the other things about it. I'm not sure precisely what's going to happen in it, but I think it's good news. Which is why I'm late."

"Acceptable," my older sister says, while my twin smothers an amused giggle.

"I'd hope so. If everything goes to plan with the cookbook, it'll be great for the bakery's sales," I point out.

"Mmm, that's true, once you know the release date we should start preparing for that. Especially if you're going to be busy. At least you can make your baklava in advance," Rowen says.

"I don't think that'll be much of a problem," I respond. "Sales of baklava are down, right?"

Oakley nods her head. "At the bakery, at least. At Cauldron Coffee, they're doing well."

"Probably because Azíl keeps telling all of Willow's customers about how good they are," Rowen says with an amused look on her face.

"He does love them." I smile as I think about our cousin's boyfriend's response to my baklava. I don't think I've ever known someone who loves it as much as he does. "But see, it's not going to be much of a problem. If we know the date, I can make a batch and that should see us through a week or so." I used to feel bad that no one likes my speciality as much as they like each of my sisters', but it doesn't bother me as much any more. Probably because I've found other things I'm good at that none of them are.

"Okay, so other than Clover's cookbook and Baklava sales being down, how are things doing?" Rowen asks.

"The children's range that Ash suggested is going strong," Oakley responds. "People are loving it, and they're often coming in with their kids to pick out treats together, so definitely worth continuing. I'd expand it too. I'm looking into some frosting techniques that could create animal-like finishes on cupcakes."

"Sounds good," Rowen says. "Though we should keep things simple when it comes to the emotions in the kids' stuff."

Oakley nods. "I'm just doing playfulness, nothing more. I don't think kids need much help in that department."

"Though parents might like it if we added some good behaviour in them," I mutter.

Hazel snickers from across the table, drawing a dirty look from Rowen. "We don't mess with people's emotions like that."

"I know, I know," my younger sister responds. "I follow the rules, you know I do."

"At least for now," I tease.

She rolls her eyes. "Only if Antonio goes through with opening his restaurant, and it'll be years before he's ready to do that."

"I can see the sign now," Oakley says. "Broomstick Restaurant."

"Wouldn't it be called DeRossi's?" Ash asks.

Hazel lets out a groan of frustration. "It's not going to be anything because it doesn't exist yet. I don't know what we'll call, or if I'll even be involved, so next time you're around Antonio, no mentioning it."

"I'm surprised you're not banning us from his company," I say.

"I can't do that, you're all invited to a party at his father's cookery school," she responds, pushing a loose strand of bright blue hair behind her ear. I'm not sure why she keeps it that colour, but it matches the fun of the macarons she makes.

"What did you have to do to get us an invite?" I ask.

"Nothing. Chef DeRossi is impressed by what we do here, you know that. So he wants us to come. And before you start nattering me about it, yes, you can bring a plus one. Even Clover."

"Hey! What's that meant to mean?" I ask.

Ash sniggers. "She's pointing out that you're the only one of us who isn't dating someone at the moment."

"Oh that." I shrug, not really caring what they think. I'm happy for my siblings, and I know that if the right person is out there for me, then I'll find them. There's nothing wrong with the fact I haven't yet. "When is it?" I ask Hazel.

"Erm, end of next month, I think. I'm not really sure. I'll get a proper invite soon and then I'll be able to tell you better."

"Good, that way we can actually plan," Rowen responds. "Do we need to do anything for it?"

"Just turn up and be your charming selves," Hazel says.

"What? You're not going to tell us we have to be on our best behaviour?" Oakley asks.

"There's no need, you'll be representing the bakery, I know none of you would even think of doing anything that would damage our reputation."

"Somehow, that makes us all sound very boring," I quip.

"Rather boring and reliable than interesting disaster zones," Oakley responds.

"Well regardless of that, I'm looking forward to going," I say. "And to seeing your other place of work."

Hazel's cheeks flush. "It's still weird to think of it that way. I can't believe I'm being paid to teach people how to bake."

"Can't you? After all the money you put into your education, I'd hope that people trusted you to teach them," Rowen says.

"*All that money?*" Hazel echoes. "I didn't see you complaining when I came back able to recreate all kinds of patisserie."

"And you won't hear me starting, they're some of our best sellers," Rowen says.

I lean back in my seat, enjoying the back and forth between my siblings. These meetings are always interesting in that they rarely actually do much other than reminding us all that we're part of a family business and that there's no escaping that.

I just wish that my part of it was more integral. Other than manning the counter, nothing that I do at the bakery actually makes a difference to the bottom line. There are some people who buy my baklava, but not nearly as many as come in for Hazel's patisserie, or Rowen's biscuits.

I push the thought to the side. It isn't the first time I've had it, and it likely won't be the last. At least I have my cookbook now. That will give me a chance to feel like I'm doing something useful. It should bring some attention to the bakery that hasn't been there before, hopefully along with some extra sales.

It's just hard when my siblings all seem to get so much out of this. Though I suppose Hazel also has her teaching job, and Oakley has the wedding cakes that she does on top of the cupcakes for the shop.

"Clover, you okay?" my little brother asks from beside me.

"Yeah, fine."

He gives me a strange look, but I dismiss it. I'm probably just reading into things because I'm feeling a little vulnerable about my place in the bakery.

"All right, I think that's everything," Rowen

says. "I need to get back to icing my biscuits. Clover, are you here or at the coffee shop tomorrow?"

"Here," I respond. "Willow said that Azíl is desperate for a day off so he's working in the front."

"What does he need a day off from?" Oakley asks.

I shrug. "I'm not sure, whatever it is he does for Sabine."

"Translations," Ash supplies.

I raise an eyebrow, surprised he knows that.

My brother shrugs. "He was telling me about it last time I did a shift there. Something about finding an ancient recipe that he wants Willow to recreate. I don't know, I didn't understand half of it."

I shake my head in bemusement, as well as affection. Willow and Azíl may only have been together for a year or so, but he's quickly become part of the family. Probably because he loves cake just as much as we do. Potentially more.

"Right, I'd better get going," Oakley says. "Justin's cooking dinner."

"I do too, I need to make sure everything's ready for my meeting," I say.

Rowen nods. "See you tomorrow, Clo."

"See you." I get to my feet and wave to my siblings, heading for the door. I love them to pieces, But I have to admit that I'm glad to be leaving.

Sometimes, it feels like my entire life has been about the bakery, and I'm glad to have something that's just mine. Even if that something is a cookbook that's *about* the bakery. So maybe it doesn't count. But at the same time, it's mine, and that's something no one can take away from me.

TWO

TYLER

I KNOCK on Dad's office door, almost dreading the conversation to come. I have no idea which client he's going to assign to me, but he normally gives me the ones that no one else will take, which means I need to prepare for someone difficult who refuses to see that sometimes creativity has to come second to logistics.

"Come in," he calls out.

I take a deep breath and push open the door, stepping inside.

"Ah, Ty, have a seat, son." He gestures to the chair opposite him, acting almost as if he isn't the one who has requested this meeting in the first place.

I don't point that out, and instead take the seat.

"We have a new client I want you to take the lead on," he says, holding a folder out to me.

I take it from him and flip it open. "A cookbook?"

He nods. "Not just any cookbook either."

"This isn't the kind of thing we normally publish," I point out.

"Yes, I know, but we've been looking to branch out and I have it on good authority that this is a sure bet." He taps the top of the folder.

I frown. "The only cookbook we've ever done was the one for Chef DeRossi, and that only did well because it had his name on it."

"Ah, and that's where this one is going to succeed too. Have you seen who the author is?"

I glance back down at the folder. "Clover Parkes? I've not heard of her." Though I'm aware that it doesn't mean anything. There are plenty of celebrities I've never met.

Dad lets out an exasperated sigh. "Her family owns Broomstick Bakery."

I raise an eyebrow. "The place Mum always gets cakes from when we have guests?"

"That's the one."

"So we're taking on this client because Mum will like it?"

Dad chuckles. "No, Ty. We're taking it on because the bakery has a huge reputation that we can tap into. There's nothing on the market like this."

"I hate to break it to you, but the market is flooded with baking books."

"Ah, but baking books where the magic is infused into the food itself?"

"Is that what they do there?" I sit back in my seat and try to recall if I'd noticed any difference in the way I felt the last time I ate one of the pastries Mum brought home. I don't think I did, but if I wasn't looking for it, then perhaps I missed it.

Or maybe it's all just the placebo effect and there's no actual magic involved. I've heard that pixie magic can work a bit like that.

"I don't know anything about baking," I say. "Are you sure I'm the right person to be doing this one?"

"This is going to be a big money-maker for us," Dad says. "I can feel it in my bones. There was a bidding war for the contract, which means that Ms Parkes has options if she decides she doesn't like us."

"Wouldn't she have to pay back her advance if she decides to do that?"

"We have to assume that she's going to. I want you to take the lead on this one because I trust you to handle it right," Dad says. "No one else has the same experience as you do, and you know it."

I let out a loud sigh. "All right. So what do I need to know?"

"For a start, you should get to know her products. Do the normal research you do when you're working with a new client. You've got a meeting with her in a couple of days..."

"I do?" I pull out my phone and pull up my calendar, surprised to find he's right. "When did you sneak that in?"

"Yesterday. If you paid more attention to your emails, you'd have seen it already."

I bite my tongue and don't reply to point out that I'm here, which means that I haven't been ignoring my emails. When that happens, he ends up coming to *my* office to get me and berate me.

"Anything else I should know?" I ask instead.

"Don't mess this up, Tyler. This is going to be a big deal for our publishing house."

"Even bigger than DeRossi?"

"It's all part of the same thing. If we can make a name for ourselves in magical food and drink, then we won't have to worry about some of the bigger publishers breathing down our necks as much."

I nod, though I have to wonder whether that's actually true. A lot of them have more money than we do, and more experience of the market. I don't think we'll ever be free from worrying about them.

"Are you coming round for dinner tonight?" Dad asks, abruptly changing the subject. "The Jungs are coming, and they're bringing their daughter."

I let out a groan. "Please tell me you're not trying to set me up with their daughter again."

"I think they said their son was free too."

"I don't want to be set up with either of them," I say. "It's not a matter of preference, just a matter of not wanting to go on a date arranged by my parents."

"So, are you coming?" Dad asks, deftly ignoring my concern.

"Yes, I'm coming. But only because Mum will be making yaksiks, and she makes it better than I can, not because I want to be set up with either of the Jungs."

Dad chuckles. "I'm sure she'll make you extra. You know she worried about you feeding yourself now you live away from home. You could move back and have food all the time."

"I'm thirty, Dad, I don't need to live at home any more."

"It's not about need, it's about family."

"I'll keep that in mind," I lie. I love my parents dearly, but the idea of living with them again fills me with an acute sense of dread. It wouldn't just be the Jungs I had to worry about them setting me up with if I'm at home, but just about everyone who lives in the neighbourhood. No matter how many times I've told them that I'm fine and that I'll meet someone when I'm ready to, they can't seem to get it through their heads. At least not since I broke up with my ex.

I push the thought to the side and close the folder about Clover Parkes and her baking book. "Well, I'll leave you to it." I get to my feet.

"Make sure you do your research before the meeting."

I let out a loud sigh. "How about I go down there now? I can pick up some stuff for Mum and do research at the same time."

"I think that's an excellent idea," Dad responds. "If they have any strawberry tarts, I wouldn't mind one myself."

"I'll see what they've got." At least it'll assure him that I'm doing my job right. Though I'm confused about why he's asking me to be the one to take Ms Parkes on as a client if he doesn't think I'm capable of that. It's probably best not to consider all of the reasoning.

I head back to the office to get my coat. It looks sunny outside, but I know better than to risk the British weather without it. And then, I guess I'm heading to the bakery.

THREE

CLOVER

THE BELL RINGS and I look up to find a handsome Asian man entering the shop with an intrigued expression on his face.

"Welcome to Broomstick Bakery," I say brightly.

"Hi," he responds.

"Can I help you with anything today?"

"My dad would like a strawberry tart, if you have any of those."

"Hmm, I don't think we have out here, but I can ask my sister if she has the stuff to make one."

"You're one of the owners?" he asks.

I nod. "Clover." I reach out my hand across the counter without thinking about it.

"I'm Tyler, it's good to meet you," he responds, taking my hand in his and giving it a shake.

His grip is warm and reassuring, without being too tight, and I have to force myself to think in terms of customer service. I clear my throat and pull my hand back. "Likewise, let me just ask Hazel. That is if you have time to wait for her to make one up?"

"I do, I'm not sure Dad would forgive me if I went back to the office without one for him."

"Oh, you're in a family business as well?"

"I am."

I smile and open the door to the kitchen. "Hazel?"

My sister pops her head around the corner. "Everything okay?"

"Have you got any strawberry tarts back there?"

"Hmm, I don't think so, but I have some raspberry ones I was about to top, I can make you up a strawberry one?"

"Please. We've got a customer asking."

"I can do that. The creme patisserie has satisfaction mixed into it," she says.

"Thanks, I'll let him know." I turn back to the

counter and smile at Tyler. "One strawberry tart coming up."

"You don't have to go to all of that trouble," he says.

"It's no trouble," I assure him. "Hazel's in the middle of putting some tarts together, so she'll just add strawberries to one of them. They're infused with satisfaction as the emotion. I hope that's okay."

"So you really infuse your cakes with emotions?" he asks.

"Mmhmm. Have you not had one before?"

"I have, but I wasn't really paying attention, so I didn't notice if they made me feel any different."

"They're not meant to change your emotions," I correct him. "Just to make you sense a different one. I can get you a sample. What kind of cake do you prefer?"

"Hmm, I'm more of a pastry person, if I'm honest. You probably don't have any baklava, that's my favourite."

My eyes light up. "Mine too." I head over to the far right of the counter. "With dates, pistachios, or walnuts? I think the ones with just honey might be ready too, but I'd prefer to let them soak for another night."

Surprise flits over his face. "You make the baklava?"

"I do. We each have something we specialise in," I say. "I make the baklava, Hazel is classically trained in patisserie. My eldest sister makes the biscuits, and my twin makes the cupcakes. She does wedding cakes too. Oh, and then there's my brother. He's still studying at the moment, but he makes a killer croissant." I can hear the excitement in my voice as I talk about each of my siblings. The business may have been a gift from our Granny, but it's our hard work that's made it into the success it is today.

"I didn't realise that, I guess I assumed you all made everything."

"It wouldn't be as good if we did," I respond. "It's better if we each focus on our own thing." I grab the tongs and pull out one each of the baklava. I cut them in half and hold out the chopping board for him.

He picks up the pistachio one first. "Are you joining me?"

"I can do. This one is infused with excitement."

"That's an interesting choice."

"I felt it went well with nuts," I respond. "But maybe you'll feel differently." I snap off my glove and drop it in the bin, knowing that I'll need a new one anyway. I pick up the piece of baklava and put it in my mouth, enjoying the nutty and sweet flavour of it. Thankfully, this does seem like it's one of my better batches.

"Oh, I feel it," Tyler says. "It's like it's jumping around my stomach."

I nod. "But it doesn't change how you're actually feeling."

"Could you do that?"

"I don't know, I've never tried," I admit. "That's not what we're trying to do here. In theory, you could make the spell stronger so it would mask someone's mood in a different way. That would mean that they weren't able to tell where their actual emotions start and the spell stops, but it would fade fairly quickly, I think."

"I can see how that would be a problem."

"Or not. I wouldn't want to *actually* mess with someone's emotions, that feels like it would be asking for trouble. And that's without thinking about the ethics of it all."

"True. So which is this one?" He picks up a second piece of baklava from the chopping board I've placed on top of the display cabinet.

"That's the date one. It's infused with warmth."

"Is warmth an emotion?"

"I guess it depends. But I based this one on the kind of warmth you feel when you spend time with someone you have a connection with. Do you know the one?"

"I think so." His dark eyes bore into me, as if he's assessing everything I'm saying on a deeper level than he should be.

My gaze is fixated on him as he lifts the baklava to his mouth and takes a bite. I don't know what it is about him, but he's certainly captured my attention, even if this meeting is only a fleeting one, and the only reason he's hanging around is because Hazel is finishing a tart for his dad.

"That one's nice," he says.

"Thank you. It's one of my favourites," I admit.

"What did you put with the walnut?" He picks up the last piece and turns it around as if hoping it's going to spill its secrets to him right there and then.

"Down-to-earthness."

"Now I think you're just making it up," he jokes.

"Aren't all spells made up?"

"That's fair, though I can't say I've ever thought about infusing the food I make with emotions."

"It takes practice," I admit. "The first time I tried, my pastry was so tough only Granny would eat it. I don't know why she did, it was really bad." I smile at the memory.

"It seems as if you've improved."

"I should hope so. I've been doing this since I left the academy."

He chuckles. "Yes, but that could be a year ago."

"Are you hoping that flattery will get you more free samples?"

"No, I really can't tell how old you are," he admits. "You could be twenty or forty-two, I wouldn't know."

"I'm not sure if I should be insulted or not by the implication that I could be in my forties."

Alarm crosses his face, as if he hadn't considered how his statement sounded out loud.

"Don't worry, I won't hold it against you. I'm twenty-seven, so somewhere between the two." Not that it really matters. I don't mind the idea that I give off at least a small air of maturity.

"I'm sorry," he murmurs.

"Seriously, I don't mind. I know what you were trying to say." I eat the last piece of baklava. "You should eat that, it'll make you feel better."

"Will it, though?"

I chuckle. "Probably not, but at least you'll have something to focus on other than your embarrassment over asking a woman her age."

He lets out a good-natured laugh. "You're not wrong there. These really are delicious by the way.

How many would you say I needed for a dinner party of eight people?"

"Erm, it depends. Are they for dessert, or for coffee?"

"Probably coffee, I don't actually know, Dad told me to get some stuff because Mum loves your cakes."

"Okay, then I'd suggest eight of the baklava. Or nine if you want three of each."

"Let's do that."

"So you can eat the leftover one?"

"Guilty as charged," he quips. "And then maybe some breakfast pastries?"

"Sure. We've got croissants, pain-aux-raisins, and I think we've got some fresh brioche buns too, they were baked this morning."

"I'll take two of everything."

"Should I be worried about what kind of party you're throwing?" The joke slips out before I can think about whether or not it's a good idea to say it.

"It isn't for me, it's for my Mum. She's having a dinner party where she's trying to set me up with the children of some of her family friends."

I raise an eyebrow. "Multiple children?" I bag up his pastries and set them on top of the counter.

He lets out a loud sigh. "She thinks that because

I refuse to be set up with the daughter, that she should try to set me up with the son."

"What's wrong with either of them?"

"Nothing, they're both lovely, attractive, and successful. I just don't want to be set up by my mum. So much so that I'm now telling a complete stranger about them."

"You know my name, I'm not a complete stranger," I point out.

He chuckles. "True. Though I'm starting to wonder whether you put a truth serum in those baklavas."

"You'll find out when your mum starts talking about things you'd rather not know about," I joke.

His amused smile is enough to make me certain that I haven't crossed a line by saying that.

The door from the kitchen opens and Hazel appears with a box. "One strawberry tart."

"Thanks, Zel."

"You're welcome."

I take the box from her and set it on the counter. "Anything else?" I ask Tyler.

"I think that's probably it for now, but I'll be back the next time I have a hankering for a baklava," he says.

A slight blush reaches my cheeks. It isn't often that someone says they want to come in for my baklava, and it's nice that's the case for him. Though I try not to read too much into it. He's just being nice, and happens to like the baking I do, nothing more than that.

I hold out the payment machine for him and wave him off, knowing that I'm probably never going to see him again, even if he says he'll be back for more baklava. It doesn't matter, I've still had a fun time interacting with him, and that's all that matters. It's moments like this that make serving behind the counter less boring and more rewarding, that's for certain.

FOUR

CLOVER

I FIDDLE with the lapel of my jacket, hoping that I look smart enough and fearing that I don't. I'm a baker, I don't have a lot of fancy clothing because I just don't have a need for it. Except that now that I have a meeting with my editor, I do.

Maybe I should have splashed out and gotten a suit for the occasion, but between my shifts at the bakery, and the ones at Willow's coffee shop, I just haven't had time. I know that I could ask any of my sisters to have covered for me, but I just didn't think of it in time.

So the blazer and smart dress combination is just going to have to do.

"Mr Kim will see you now," the receptionist says, gesturing to the row of doors.

"Thank you." I get to my feet and smooth down my dress, hoping there aren't many wrinkles in it from sitting down.

I read the names on each of the doors, trying not to focus on the incessant nerves bouncing around my stomach. I've never been in this kind of meeting before and I don't know what to expect.

I stop in front of a door with the plaque *Mr T Kim* on it and raise my fist to knock.

"Come in," a semi-familiar voice calls. But that doesn't mean anything. I interact with a lot of people on a daily basis, it could be anyone on the other side of the door.

I open it and step inside, stopping in my tracks when the man lifts his head and I recognise him instantly. "Tyler?"

"Good morning, Clover," he says, not seeming anywhere near as surprised as I am.

"You knew who I was when you came into the bakery," I say, not moving from my spot by the door.

"I didn't know exactly who you were, but I did know that it was your bakery, yes."

"Why didn't you tell me?" I ask.

"Do you want the answer that makes me sound good as an editor, or the truth?"

"Both?" Despite the annoyance within me, I have to admit that I'm a little intrigued.

A smile lifts the corners of his lips. "That's an interesting answer."

"I'm an interesting person."

"So I'm starting to realise. Please, take a seat." He gestures to the empty chair on this side of his desk.

Despite my trepidation, I sit down. "So, which answer is it?"

"Well, the answer that makes me sound like a good editor is that I was going there on a mystery shopper trip so that I could get a sense of what the bakery has to offer and what I could expect from us working together. Telling you who I was would have defeated the point."

"And the truth?"

"I forgot. I had every intention of introducing myself, but I got distracted by our conversation."

"That just sounds like flattery."

"It wasn't meant to. I was telling the truth when I said I'd had your cakes before but not tried them properly, I was intrigued about what they might be like. I appreciated how much care and attention you took in helping me make the best choices. If all of your customers receive that kind of service, I can see how you've built such a strong business."

I narrow my eyes at him. "Now I know that's flattery."

"I promise it's not empty. I mean everything I say."

"Hmm."

"And everything else I told you was true too. My parents really are trying to set me up with the children of a family friend, and this is a family business."

"You just failed to mention that it was the family business that's offered me a publishing contract." I cross my arms.

"Should I have given you my business card right then and there?"

"Yes."

"Then let me rectify that." He picks one up from his desk and holds it out to me.

I eye him warily, but reach out to take it all the same.

"So, do you have any questions for me?" he asks.

"Did your parents successfully set you up?"

He chuckles. "Is that your way of asking if I'm single?"

"I don't need to ask that, if they're trying to set you up, then the answer is yes."

"Astute. But no, I escaped unharmed."

"You must be so pleased."

"I am," he responds. "Especially as my mum was very pleased with the pastries I brought her, I have you to thank for that."

"I'm glad I could help."

"Even if I gained information on your pastries by deception?"

"You claimed that it was an accident that you didn't disclose who you were Mr Kim."

"You should call me Tyler, we're going to be spending a lot of time together," he responds.

"Ms Parkes will do here." I can't keep a straight face even as I say it. "Scrap that, I promise Clover is fine. Ms Parkes sounds so formal."

"You'll have to get used to it if you're going to be doing interviews and TV segments for your cookbook."

I grimace. "Is that really going to happen?"

"Probably not for the launch," he admits. "But if you hit the sales projections that my father set out for you, then it's a real possibility."

"Dare I ask about them?"

"Do you want to know?"

I frown. Do I? "Honestly, I'm not sure they'll mean anything to me if you tell me," I admit.

"Then they can stay a secret between me and this folder." He pats the top of it.

I let out a small laugh. "What other secrets do you and your folder have?"

"Only ones pertaining to my dating life."

"Oh, so you're not going to keep mentioning things in off-handed ways to me about that then?" Why am I enjoying myself so much? I barely know this guy, and here I am having some kind of weird back and forth with him.

At least it's fun, I guess that isn't what I expected when I found out that I had to have a meeting with my editor. I expected more of a going through everything with a red pen and a fine tooth comb situation.

Maybe that's coming.

"So what should I expect?" I ask. "This is my first time doing anything like this."

"Is this where I say it's my first time too?" he jokes.

"Is it?"

"No. I started working for my father as soon as I left the academy, I've been doing this for over five years."

"Ah, so you're not forty-two either?"

"I'm not."

"See, I do think you're dropping hints at me again about how eligible you are. You're talking about your stable job, your age, the fact that your parents clearly adore you and think you're a catch..."

"Aren't all parents supposed to think that?"

I shrug. "Mine have never tried to set me up with anyone."

"I suspect they also encouraged you to find a passion instead of doing what looked good too?"

"They did. Are you saying that you don't want to be an editor?"

"Actually, I do," he says. "In this case, I was lucky that what I wanted, and what they wanted were the same thing."

"That is handy," I agree.

"I started working for Dad because I wanted to. He loved his strawberry tart, by the way. And was very impressed that it was made especially for him."

"He probably thinks I'm trying to bribe him now."

"That would only have been the case if you'd brought another one with you today."

"If I'd realised who I was visiting, maybe I would have done."

"And some baklava?" The way his face lights up

makes me think that he's serious about his love for it.

"Nope, you didn't disclose who you were, so no baklava for you."

"That's fair," Tyler responds. "Though now that I've told you the truth, perhaps you might reconsider about that and bring me some next time?"

"Wouldn't that be considered bribery?"

"We've already paid you your advance," he points out. "So I don't think there's anything to bribe us over."

"Then I suppose next time we come for a meeting, I'll bring some baklava. Any preferences for what kind?"

"Surprise me."

"And the emotion?"

"You can surprise me with that too."

"What if I brought something you didn't like?"

"Such as?"

"Fear, loathing, disgust..."

"It's just sounding like the end of a bad date now."

I snort. "I wouldn't put those into any cakes anyway."

"I know you wouldn't, and somehow I can say that with certainty despite the fact we've only just met," Tyler responds. "But I trust your discretion when it comes to choosing what's in them."

"You should be more careful or I'll bring some of my sister's midsummer flirt cupcakes."

He raises an eyebrow. "That just seems like an excuse to flirt."

"Considering it's how she met her boyfriend, you might be right about that."

"Then is this your way of telling me that you want me to flirt with you? Because I can assure you, I don't need any kind of cupcakes to do that." He shoots me a lopsided grin.

"We shouldn't mix business with flirting," I murmur, as much as I like the idea of flirting with him.

He sighs. "You're right. So then, let's get down to business. We've got a lot to get through." The change in his demeanour is instantaneous, and I'm already regretting my words. But now that I've said them, there's no going back, and I know it's for the best if we don't allow ourselves to get distracted by anything as unprofessional as flirting, even if it does sound a lot less fun.

FIVE

Clover

I HUM to myself as I clean up the displays ready for the morning. It always amazes me how dirty they seem to get. I'd never have known that cake left so much dirt around before we took over the bakery from Granny. But there's no doubt that what's in front of me is a mess.

The door opens, and I look up, half expecting it to be a customer I have to turn away, but it isn't. "Hey Justin," I say to my twin's boyfriend. "I think Oakley's in the back sorting out her wedding cake for tomorrow."

"I actually came to talk to you first," he says.

"She's loading up the van already, so I don't have long."

"Okay, what is it?" I ask, admittedly a little confused by why he wants me and not the person he's actually dating.

He takes a deep breath, nerves written all over his face. "I want to ask Oakley to marry me," he blurts out.

My eyes widen. "You want to propose?"

He nods. "I know it's quick..."

"It's been nine months," I say. "In Oakley's romance time, that's more like nine years." Which is probably a bit of an exaggeration, but he's dating my sister, he's well aware of what a hopeless romantic she is, otherwise he wouldn't have fallen for her.

"I don't know whether you're trying to tell me it's too soon, or if I should have done it sooner," he admits.

"I think you're right on time," I assure him.

"Good, because I thought about waiting, but then I saw the ring, and I just knew that it was right. You know?"

"I really don't," I point out. "I'm neither engaged, or proposing to anyone."

He chuckles. "That's fair."

40

"What did you need my help for? I don't think it's traditional to ask the twin sister for permission."

"It's not, though I'm presuming that if I didn't have your approval, I'd have been kicked to the curb long ago."

"In theory, but you know Oakley, once her mind is made up about something, nothing will change it, even common sense."

"Which is how she ended up dating that idiot for so long."

I snort. "If you're already thinking of Craig as *that idiot*, then you definitely fit right in here. Though that might be tame compared to the words Rowen uses for him."

"Good to know. So I guess I wanted to ask how you thought it was best to do it. She's talked so much about the wedding and the marriage she wants, but she's never once said anything about what she wants for her proposal. I've tried to bring it up, but she just says something vague about knowing when she knows."

"She's testing you, Justin," I say. "Well, kind of. She's avoiding answering because whether you propose in the right will tell her how well you know her."

"I feared as much. I don't think she'll want anything big or flashy, but every time I think that, I start second-guessing myself and wondering whether or not I'm right."

"You are," I assure him. "She hates the idea of a public proposal, she says that it would make her feel like she had to say yes, even if she didn't want to."

"See, that's what I thought."

"Then you're doing just fine. You know her well and the two of you are good together, just trust your instincts."

"So favourite flower, favourite dinner, ring."

I nod. "That sounds like Oak."

"Yeah, it does." He sighs.

"Do you have the ring with you?" I ask, my curiosity getting the better of me.

He puts his hand in his pocket and pulls out a black velvet ring box. He holds it out to me and pops the lid. Inside sits a ring that screams Oakley. She's going to love it.

"It's perfect."

"I thought so." He runs a hand through his dark hair, clearly a little nervous. "I don't want her to think I'm rushing things."

"So long as you're not planning on getting married tomorrow, I think you're fine," I assure him.

"No, that's not the plan."

I shrug. "Then you're fine, Oakley loves you, she'll be over the moon when you ask."

"Thanks, Clover, I appreciate it."

I smile reassuringly at my future brother-in-law. I guess I've actually been thinking about him like that for a while, but this time it feels real.

The door to the kitchen opens and he fumbles with the box, snapping it closed and shoving it back into his pocket.

I turn in time to see Oakley step in, her face lighting up when she sees her boyfriend. "I didn't realise you'd arrived." She leans over the counter and kisses him on the cheek.

He nods. "I was just coming to talk to Clover about some baklava," he lies.

Oakley gives him a weird look, but shrugs. "I'm nearly ready to go. I've got everything in the van already."

"Did you remember to test the frosting?" he asks, half-teasing, half-serious. After the mishap at his sister's wedding, I doubt he's ever going to let her live down the fact that she accidentally made the frosting taste of thunder instead of newly-wed-bliss. It wasn't Oakley's finest moment, but she did find love as a result, so I suppose she can't complain too much.

"I tested the frosting," she assures him. "And I saved you a tester just in case."

"Wise," he responds.

She rolls her eyes. "Why don't you come on back? Rowen's just finishing up on her biscuit order for that kids' party, but it isn't too hectic back there."

"Are you dropping those off too?" I ask her.

She shakes her head. "I think the parents are coming in tomorrow to pick them up."

"Ah, that must be one of the notes Rowen left on the till." I flick through them, finding the one in question. "Right, the Fields' order."

Oakley nods. "That sounds familiar. They're looking good, the biscuits are all shaped like farm animals and when you eat them, you make the noise of the animal."

I raise an eyebrow. "Rowen agreed to make those?"

"Apparently, I was surprised too, but you know she's been talking of expanding recently. I think she's taking that idea seriously," my twin responds.

"Interesting."

"I think they'll be a real hit with the kids."

"I can see that. It could also mean more events for Rowen. Can you imagine how well they'd sell at the Staffordshire Show?"

"Oh, yes, we should suggest that to her. I know she keeps saying that she wants a stall in the Food

Hall there, she thinks it'll be good exposure," Oakley says. "It's probably too late for this year."

"Probably, but we'll convince her to go," I respond.

"Let's hope she listens to us."

"You could just get Edward to convince her," Justin suggests. "I'm pretty sure he said something about his family vineyard having a stall there."

"Crafty, but not unreasonable," I respond. "We'll see how we get on first, and if we have to get him involved with some numbers, then that can just back up our cause." Numbers are always the best way to convince Rowen of anything.

"Right, we should get going or they'll close the venue before I can deliver this cake," Oakley says. "I'll see you later, Clo."

"See you." I wave them both off, a content feeling within me as they leave. She's going to love the proposal Justin has in mind. But I should have asked him when he was planning on doing it so I can prepare for over-excited Oakley.

And put some champagne on ice. We're going to need it.

SIX

TYLER

THERE ARE BETTER ways I can think of spending a Friday night than at an event for one of our clients, but Chef DeRossi is far too important of a client for me to miss this, especially as Dad's busy tonight with some other event that needs his attention, I think for one of Mum's charity, but I didn't ask too many questions. He might be my dad, but he's also my boss, and I know better than to go against a request from him.

I head over to the bar and look down the menu, surprised to find its mostly fancy cocktails.

"Hey, can I have a raspberry mojito, please?" a familiar voice asks.

I snap my head in that direction, surprised to find the brunette witch who has been occupying a lot of my thoughts lately leaning against the bar in a form-fitting green dress.

"Clover?"

She turns to me and smiles, flicking her hair over her shoulder. "Hey, I didn't expect to see you here." The bartender sets her drink down in front of her. "Thanks."

"Just a beer, please," I say when he approaches me.

The man nods and produces a bottle. I thank him and turn my attention to the beautiful woman at the bar.

"Chef DeRossi is one of our clients," I explain.

"Ah, I remember my agent saying that. She used it as a reason that she thought you'd be a good fit."

"I didn't realise that. So how come you're here? Did you study at the school?" I know I shouldn't pry, but I'm curious about exactly what she's doing here.

"Oh, not even slightly, but my sister did. Though that's not how we got our invite. It's actually because she's dating DeRossi Junior." She nods her head in the direction of the blue-haired woman I recognise from the bakery and the son of our client.

"I had no idea."

"Why would you? It's not exactly newsworthy information," she points out.

"Are your other siblings here too?" I ask, realising that I have no idea what the others look like.

"Yes. My brother is over by the giant croissant with his girlfriend, and that's my eldest sister at the buffet. My twin is here somewhere too." She looks around the room. "Ah, yes, she's talking with Chef DeRossi now."

"You have a twin?"

The slight amused smile on her face seems almost devious. "So despite your little mystery shopper trip, your research into me hasn't been that thorough then."

"Erm..."

"I regret telling you she was my twin, we could have played all kinds of mind games on you," she jokes.

"Have you ever done that?"

"What? Pretended to be Oakley? Of course, but not for years. Our parents encouraged us to develop our own styles and interests pretty early on, which made it easy for people to tell us apart."

"So no matching dresses and pigtails?"

"No, because we're not seven," I point out. "So, that's my family, what about yours? You work for your father, is he here?"

"It's just me tonight," he responds.

"Ah, what a shame."

"I'm sure you'll meet them at some point. Dad's in charge of the publishing company, as you know, and my sister works in the legal department."

"A true family business then."

He chuckles. "She always refused to join until after she finished law school and realised that this was what she wanted to specialise in."

"At least it means you can rely on her."

"Yes, but you never want to get into an argument with her, she'll run circles around you."

"Then if I ever need a meeting with your legal department, I'm going to drag you along with me so that you can whisper her weaknesses in my ear," she jokes.

"If I'm going to whisper in your ear, it's not going to be information about my sister," I respond without thinking it through.

"Oh? And what are you going to whisper to me?" There's a hint of challenge in her voice.

Seeing my chance, I lean in and brush her hair away from her ear. Her breathing hitches, making me question myself and what I'm doing. I'm not normally like this, but something about her brings out this side of me.

"Your baklava is better than Chef DeRossi's," I whisper.

She lets out an amused laugh. "I have to say, I'm disappointed," she responds. "I thought you were going to say something far more scandalous."

"Considering we're at a party celebrating the man, I'd say that's at least a little scandalous."

"Next time, I'll need you to try harder." She bites her bottom lip.

"Would you like a canapé?" a server asks, holding out a tray to the two of us and stopping me from answering Clover's remark.

Which is probably for the best, I don't think I could come up with a response that doesn't make it sound like I'm coming onto her.

Though perhaps I am. I should be doing the rounds of the room and making sure I speak to all of the people who matter, and instead, I just want to spend my time with her.

Though I suppose considering the fact she's our client too, it's not a bad use of my time.

Except that she *is* our client, which is something I need to remember. I can't go around flirting with her just because I find her engaging.

"Tyler?" Clover says.

I look at her, confused about what's going on.

"Do you want one?" She gestures to the tray.

"Oh, yes, please." I take one of the canapés from the server, who disappears off to serve the next people.

"What do you think it is?" Clover asks, studying the small puff pastry carefully. "I can't tell. That's always the problem with these things. They're so small that there's no way of knowing unless you made them yourself."

"Not a fan of tiny pastries?" I ask.

"No. They need to be big enough to enjoy." She pops the canapé into her mouth. "Though that's delicious."

I eat my own, not at all surprised to discover that she's right. "It's good."

"I still don't know what it is."

"Me neither, but I wouldn't be mad if they came round again."

"We can move into the path of the server again," she suggests, gesturing across the room with her half-empty glass.

"Devious."

"But fun, right?" The way she smiles makes me want to know more about her.

No, not more. *Everything.* There's something

about this woman that makes me want to spend as much time with her as possible, and it's not just because she looks hot in the dress she's wearing.

"Where's your wand?" I blurt.

"What?"

I grimace. "Sorry, ignore me."

"No, I'm interested now. Why does it matter where my wand is?" Something about her expression makes me think that she knows precisely why I'm asking.

"I guess I've always wondered where people keep them when they're wearing a dress like yours."

"A dress like mine how?" Her lips curve up into a knowing smile, like she's caught me appreciating her.

"I don't think there's a safe way to answer that," I murmur.

Clover chuckles. "No, not really. Where's yours?"

I open my jacket and pull my wand out of the specially-made pocket in the lining. "How did you know I'm a warlock?"

"A couple of things you said, and because I know your company is run by a warlock and you said he was your dad. I took a guess that your mum isn't one of the few supernatural types with stronger

DNA than warlocks, which means that you'd be one yourself."

"Impressive reasoning."

"Not really." She reaches for the bow on her belt and draws out her wand before slipping it back inside. "It's here."

"I have to admit, I'm disappointed."

"Were you expecting a thigh holster?" she asks. "Or maybe hoping for one?"

"Would you have shown me that's where your wand was if it had been?"

"You'll never know," she teases.

Someone calls her name from across the room.

"I think that's my cue to go," she says. "But it was nice seeing you outside the office, Tyler. We should do it again."

I nod, not knowing how else to respond to that.

She heads over in the direction of her family, looking over her shoulder to smile at me as she does.

It's safe to say that Clover isn't a normal client. And that the next few months are going to be interesting while we get her book ready for publishing.

If I'm not careful, I'm going to end up snared in a witch's web. And I'm not going to care even a little bit.

SEVEN

CLOVER

I OPEN the door to Tyler's office, trying not to overthink about the meeting to come, or what I expect from it. Even though I know I shouldn't, I've been replaying the conversation we had at DeRossi's party over and over again in my head. I should be keeping things professional with him, especially when he's in a position where he's in charge of getting my book into print.

And yet every time I see him, I find myself completely forgetting that.

"Hey," I say as I walk inside and take a seat opposite his desk. My stomach is fluttering like crazy, though these nerves are different from the first time I was here. They're nothing to do with the meeting itself and all to do with him. I want to know what he's thinking, and if he's as affected by me as I am by him.

Somehow, I get the idea that the answer is yes, but we both know that we shouldn't do anything about it.

"Right on time," Tyler says.

"I did consider being fashionably late, but I thought that would make a bad impression." Which is a lie. The real reason is that I didn't want to waste a moment of time I could spend talking with him.

"I don't think you could make a bad impression on anyone," he responds.

"I could try."

He chuckles. "I'm sure you could."

"So, what do you have in store for me today?" I ask.

"I wanted to check some layout ideas with you. I've been talking to the graphics department and they've sent three over for you to choose from."

"I get to choose?"

"Within reason."

"Okay, let's see, then."

He pulls out his wand and flicks it to the side.

Three panels appear there, each showing a different recipe layout.

I get to my feet and start to look at each of them in detail.

"What do you think?" he asks.

"I don't like this one at all." I point to the one on the left. "There's something about it that just feels wrong."

He nods and draws his wand down, making it vanish. "The note on the email said that one would probably be better for savoury dishes."

"Not the right choice, then."

"Did you not want to include any savouries in yours?" he asks. "I looked through the recipes you've submitted already and noticed that there weren't any."

"I have some saved at home," I admit. "But it felt like there were too few of them compared to the other sections. I could add them back in if you think the book needs them."

He shakes his head and gets to his feet to come and look at the layouts alongside me. "You can save them for if we do a second one."

"You're already considering that?"

He pauses. "I don't know how to answer that."

"Honestly."

"I can't promise anything, and we won't know

whether there's the interest for doing a second one until after this one has been released."

"Understandable. I wouldn't expect it to be any other way."

"But I hope that there will be."

"Because it'll make a lot of money for you?" I turn around, not realising quite how close it brings the two of us.

I don't move away.

"If it makes a lot of money, then it'll be for Dad and not necessarily for me," he says.

"So you're motivated by something other than the money?" I bite my bottom lip, not sure why I find the idea of that so appealing.

His gaze drops there, and I realise *exactly* why I think it is.

Without meaning to, I lean in, bringing us even closer together than we already were. My breathing intensifies and the atmosphere in the room becomes much more charged than I expect it to.

Neither of us says anything, I don't think we're capable of it. I know that this isn't what we should be doing, or what the meeting is about, but a large part of me is longing to know what it would be like to kiss him.

I reach out and place my hand on his chest, feeling his heart racing under my palm and leaving absolutely no doubt in my mind that he's feeling the intensity of the situation just as much as I am.

He clears his throat. "We shouldn't?"

"Shouldn't what?" I ask, looking up at him and seeing something warring across his face.

To my surprise, Tyler steps back and shakes his head. "I'm sorry."

I stare at him for a moment. "Right, the book," I mumble, turning around to face the layouts again. I study them while trying to calm myself and not think about what could have happened.

Frustratingly, the strongest emotion I seem to be feeling about that is disappointment.

"I think this one is better," I say, pointing to the layout on the left. "But I prefer the ingredients list on the other one, I think it's clearer to read, and that's probably something that the people using the book are going to be looking for."

He nods. "I'll let the graphics department know."

"Will that be okay? Or do I need to just get on board with this being what it'll look like?" I ask, gesturing to the one I prefer.

"It should be fine," he says, moving back around to the other side of his desk and pulling his keyboard closer. He types something out, which I assume is the email to the person in charge of graphics. "Any other requests?"

"This section here, what's it for?" I point to what almost looks like it's supposed to be a sticky note.

"Ah, that's for if you want to write any personal notes on a recipe. Things like suggestions for making it different, or if there's a tip you have for the bake. We'll put them in a handwriting font..."

"Why not just have them in my handwriting?" I ask. "Wouldn't that be a better touch? Or I could do one better and get my siblings to write them for their specialities."

"Have you included any of those in the book?"

"Kind of. I can make everything I've submitted the recipes for myself, but when it comes to shortcrust pastry, Hazel makes it much better than I can. And I simply can't make biscuits as well as Rowen, or make frosting turn out the way Oakley can." Pride fills me as I talk about my sisters.

"What about your brother?"

"Oh, I can't make croissants at all. Ash has me beaten in that regard."

"But baklava is made of pastry."

"I know, you'd think that I'd be able to make other things with it too, but trust me when I say that you don't want to eat croissants that I make, they're not good."

"I'll remember that," he says. "I'll suggest it to

graphics and see what they say. I can't promise anything though."

"That's fine, I don't expect you to." I lapse into silence, trying not to feel too awkward about what almost happened. I know it's better if we keep things professional, but I can't seem to shake the feeling that would be a mistake, even if I'm not entirely sure *why* I think that. "Is there anything else?"

"I don't think so," he responds, seeming as uncomfortable as I am. "But I'll let you know in time for our next meeting."

"Thanks." I get to my feet, pausing while I consider whether I want to say anything else. Instead of doing that, I simply smile.

He meets my gaze, and I can see the conflict lingering there. I don't know how long we're going to be able to work together and not act on the attraction that seems to be there between us, but we're going to have to try.

EIGHT

CLOVER

IT'S ALMOST EERIE to be in the bakery on my own at this time of night, but with everything on my plate, this is the only time I actually have to bake. Between the book, my shifts at Willow's coffee shop, and working the counter here, there's just so much going on that there never seems to be any time.

At least it's enough to keep my mind off Tyler.

Mostly.

Despite all of my attempts to keep my thoughts away from him, he keeps floating back into them and I find myself wondering what it would have been like if we'd actually kissed. I don't know for sure that's where we were heading, but I could feel something in the air between us, and I don't think I'm imagining it.

"Pull yourself together, Clover," I mutter to myself as I measure honey into a pot. I need to soak the baklava I made the other day, cool the pastry sheets that are currently in the oven, and make several fillings. Somehow, I'm behind on it all.

The timer trills, announcing that the sheets in the oven are done. I set down the honey, knowing that time is of the essence if I want to make sure that they aren't overdone, that could undermine the entire dish.

I grab the oven cloth I've been using and pull open the door. A hot gush of dry air rushes over my face and I wait for a moment before removing the first tray and place it on the stovetop. I wouldn't be able to do that if my sisters were also using the kitchen, but they're all out living their own lives.

I return to the oven for the second tray, accidentally brushing my arm against the wire rack above it. I flinch and pull my arm back, hissing as I do. My arms are covered in marks from where I've burned myself before, but somehow it never actually stops hurting when I do it.

I push through the pain and grab the other two

trays of pastry. What's a little pain compared to ruined baked goods? I drop them onto the top and turn the oven down so it's ready for when I need to bake my fillings, before heading over to the sink to run my new burn under cold water. It's already turned bright red and is starting to pull at the pale skin around it.

The cold water both soothes and hurts at the same time. "Ahhh."

"Clover?"

I twist around to see Rowen entering the kitchen wearing a comfortable-looking dressing gown.

"Sorry, I didn't mean to disturb you," I say.

"You didn't. I was about to make us some rum toddies but I've run out of milk, I thought I'd come pilfer some from the fridge," she responds.

"Edward's here?" I can't keep the surprise out of my voice. I never thought Rowen would be so quick to settle into the habits of an established relationship, but she has done.

"The flat's closer to his new client's office than his house is."

"Mmhmm, he's here for purely practical reasons, nothing else." It's impossible to keep the amusement out of my voice.

"Is the burn bad?" she asks, gesturing to the sink and ultimately changing the subject completely.

I sigh. "I've had worse."

"Sit down, I'll help you with it. You know my healing magic is better than yours."

"I just never got the hang of it." I shut off the tap and head over to the seating area in the corner. "Maybe because you and Mum always insisted on helping us so I didn't practise already."

"More likely it's just not the type of magic you excel at," she reminds me. "Didn't you say you've really taken to the defensive magic you've been learning with Willow?"

I nod. "It seems to come fairly easily."

"So there you have it, you're a fighter, not a healer." She gestures for me to hold my arm out, taking it in her hand once I do and examining the burn. "Not too bad," she agrees.

"I told you as much."

She shakes her head in bemusement and pulls out her wand. She points it towards the burn and an immediate sense of comfort spreads over the area. It'll still be burned once she's done, but it should be enough to start the healing process and mean that I don't have to go through the most painful part of it.

"This is what you get for baking so late at night," she says.

"You don't have to tell me that," I mutter. "I'm well aware."

"So why are you doing it?"

"Because when else am I going to?"

"You've taken too much on," she says astutely.

I sigh and lean back in my seat. "I know I have, but I don't want to give any of it up."

She nods. "That's not it, though, is it?"

"What do you mean?"

"You've never been very good at hiding when something's bothering you. So out with it."

"You're getting bossy in your old age."

"One, I'm not old. Two, I've always been bossy," my big sister responds. "So spill."

I sigh. "It's going to sound ridiculous."

"Try me."

"So you know I've been having meetings about my cookbook?"

"You said they've been going well," she responds.

"And they have. The only thing is that I guess I've kind of been flirting with my editor."

Rowen chuckles. "So that's why they've been going well?"

"Actually, I think they've been going well despite that. Every time I think that it might be something to explore, it's like he remembers that we're supposed to be working together and clams up."

"Have you seen him outside of a work environment?"

I frown, thinking through my interactions with Tyler. "Maybe not?"

"Then there's your problem. You should message him and ask him out to dinner or something. Anything that's not to do with work."

"Do you really think that's a good idea? What if things go badly and we end up making working together really awkward?"

Rowen shrugs. "Isn't it going to be anyway if you're thinking about him that way?"

"Eurgh, I hate it when you're right."

"That's a lie. If you hated it, you wouldn't come to me for advice."

"I hate it despite the fact it's useful when you give it," I respond.

Rowen's smug smile is enough to have me shaking my head.

"You're the best big sister I could have asked for," I admit.

"I'm glad you think so."

"What, you're not going to tell me that I'm the best little sister?" I joke.

"And risk Hazel and Oakley finding out? No thank you."

I chuckle. "All right, that's fair."

"Are you going to be okay if I go back upstairs?" she asks.

I nod. "I'll be fine. And I'll be more careful with the oven for the rest of the night."

"You'd better be," she responds. "I don't want to have to keep coming down to do healing spells on you."

"Say hi to Edward for me."

"I will." She smiles and goes to the fridge to grab herself the milk she came down for then heads up to the flat. I'm not sure I could do what she does and live above the bakery, but I know it suits her well.

I pull out my phone and hover my finger above Tyler's contact information. I click on it before I lose my nerve and type out a quick message. I half wish that Rowen was still here to make sure I hit send, but I don't need her to do that.

I drop my phone onto the table the moment the message is sent and get to my feet so I can turn my attention back to the baklava I'm in the middle of making. At least I have that to distract myself while I wait for Tyler to reply.

If he's going to.

I push that thought aside. I'm not imagining things, there's a connection between us, now it's just up to the two of us to act on it and hope that we're not making a terrible mistake.

NINE

TYLER

I ARRIVE at the restaurant and run my finger around the neck of my shirt, trying not to worry too much about the dinner I'm about to have. I'm not sure whether Clover meant to ask me here on a business dinner, or on a date, but I'm trying to be prepared for either despite knowing which I really want.

I take a deep breath and head inside.

"Good evening, sir," the maitre'd says as I approach.

"Evening," I respond. "I'm meeting someone here."

"Do you have a reservation?" he asks.

"I think it'll be under Parkes."

He nods. "Right this way, sir, the rest of your party is already here." He turns and starts to lead me through the crowded restaurant. It certainly has a date-like air to it. I think it's the candlelight and the soft music playing.

Clover looks up from where she's sitting at one of the tables, her face lighting up when she sees me. She gets to her feet, revealing a black dress that definitely doesn't look like it belongs at a business meeting. "You came," she says.

"I said I would."

"Right, of course."

Is it me, or does she seem a little flustered?

"Your server will be with you shortly," the maitre'd says with a nod of his head.

"Thank you," Clover responds, not taking her eyes off me as she does.

A part of me wants to lean in and kiss her cheek. Or just kiss her properly. I haven't been able to think of anything else since our almost kiss in my office, it's been all-consuming and highly distracting. I've never felt like this about someone before. Or at least, I don't think I have. It's certainly more intense than anything I think I've shared with another person.

"I don't think I've ever been here before," I say, looking around and trying to work out if that's true.

"Me neither, but my cousin recommended it. Her partner loves trying new restaurants, so she's tried most of them in the area."

"Is her partner not local?" I ask.

Clover lets out a small laugh. "You could say that."

"Cryptic."

"He's Moroccan. Kind of. It's a long story," she says. "And not really mine to tell."

"Fair enough. You're close with your cousin, then?"

She nods. "I do shifts at her coffee shop too."

"Should I be worried about your family taking over the town with all of your businesses?"

"Absolutely."

I let out a bemused laugh at her response.

"Not what you expected?"

"I think it's safe to say that you're not what I thought you were going to be," I admit.

"Dare I ask?"

"Well, when I think of bakers, I think of that little old lady who does the baking shows on TV."

"That little old lady is an icon," Clover reminds me. "She may be human, but she's still got magic."

"Her cakes do always look delicious," I agree.

"So did your cousin make any suggestions about what to eat here?" I ask, picking up the menu.

"No, but her partner said that he likes the slow-roasted lamb with the tender stem broccoli and finished off with a strawberry pavlova."

"That's a very specific order."

"No one gets between Azíl and his food," she responds with an affectionate smile on her face.

"Which coffee shop is it that your cousin owns?" I ask.

"Cauldron Coffee Shop. It's not far from the bakery."

"I've seen it. I think some of our interns have gone on coffee runs there."

"I'm not surprised, Willow loves her coffee, she always makes sure that it's the best she can get her hands on."

"And you said you work there?"

"Mostly as a favour to her," Clover admits. "She had some problems with one of her baristas, so I stepped in and helped out a few times, but it turns out that I actually enjoy it, so I've kept at it even though she needs me less."

"You're a busy woman," I say. "I should be honoured that you're free to have dinner with me."

"You should," she agrees. "But it's hardly a chore

for me. I enjoy good company." The expression on her face makes it clear that she means the words.

"Then I'm even more honoured that you think I'm good company. I hope you still think as much by the end of the night."

"I think that will depend on how well you know your wine," she says. "I have no idea where to start with the wine menu."

"So there *is* something that you're not good at."

"You'll find that there's plenty of things, I just avoid doing them so no one knows."

"Like what?"

"I'm *really* bad at languages. My cousin and siblings can all speak an extra one or two each, but me? I'm just really bad at it, I could never pick it up. What about you?"

"I can't say the same, I'm bi-lingual."

She raises an eyebrow. "Which languages?"

"English and Korean. Dad's a second-generation immigrant, but Mum's Korean and came across when she was thirteen, so they both spoke it at home when I was younger. We still speak it at home when we're the only ones there."

"That's amazing, I've always envied people who are brought up bilingual. It must be so cool to be able to switch between languages."

"Sometimes. It's fun when you have lots of different ways to insult your sister all at once."

She lets out an amused laugh. "I can see that." The way she smiles makes something light up inside me. "So, do you know anything about wine?"

"I know not to order the cheapest one."

"That's the kind of information I need when I'm at a restaurant."

"And that if we're going to eat lamb, then we should probably go for a red."

"Are we sharing a bottle now?" she asks.

"Would you like to?" It feels as if I'm asking about more than just the wine, but I can't quite put my finger on what it is that I'm saying.

"I think that sounds like a good idea," she responds. "It wouldn't be wise to drink a bottle on my own anyway, who knows what I might say."

"Couldn't you just brew yourself up a sobering potion?"

"What makes you think that I don't have one waiting for me at home?" Clover asks.

"Do you?"

"No. But I do have a hangover cure. It's best to always be prepared for these kinds of things."

"Mmm, that's true. I should really learn from you and stock up on them. I don't think I have a single hangover cure in my medicine cabinet."

"You're a warlock, you could make one yourself."

"True, but I learned my lesson about trying to brew things when I'm either drunk or hungover when I was at the academy."

"What happened?" She leans forward, the flowery scent of her perfume filling the air around her as she does.

"I'm not sure I want to say," I admit, thinking about how the answer might not make me seem like an appealing prospect to the beautiful woman in front of me.

"How about I'll trade an embarrassing story of me at the academy for information about what happened when you tried to brew a potion when hungover?"

"All right, but it had better be of equal embarrassingness."

"I promise to do my best," she responds.

"I was supposed to be trying to brew a potion for teeth-whitening..."

"Interesting choice."

"One of my friends told me that no one would be interested in someone unless their teeth sparkled like the stars," I explain.

"That sounds like a lie."

"Oh, it definitely was. He was just trying to

make it so that my mouth was glittery. I'm not sure
if it was a prank, or to make him look better.
Anyway, I was hungover when I tried to make it, or
maybe I was still drunk, you know what those
parties are like at the academy."

"I do, I had my share of still-drunk-the-next-
morning moments," she admits. "What happened
with your potion?"

"I drank it, and I must have gotten something
wrong, because I turned glittery everywhere. It was
like my skin was made of tiny mirrors."

She laughs, then covers her mouth with her
hand. "I'm sorry, I know that I shouldn't find that
funny."

I shrug. "But it is."

"Which academy did you go to? You're the same
age as Rowen, I'm surprised I haven't heard that
story."

"I went to Hexington Academy," he says.

"Ah, we went to Grimalkin."

"You didn't go far down the road then."

"No, it's a good academy and I suppose none of
us really saw the need to. We were already helping
Granny out at the bakery sometimes by that point
too, so it made sense for us to stay."

"Understandable. Now, your embarrassing
story?" I prompt.

"Hmmm, I'm not sure I have one as good as glitter-skin, though I think you'd make a fortune if you still had the recipe for that potion still."

"Sadly, I have no clue what I did wrong to have that result."

"That's a real shame. You could have been a millionaire. Then again, I suppose you're the heir to a publishing fortune."

"I wouldn't go that far. The publishing house does well, but it's not going to make me a millionaire."

The server arrives and we place our food order, barely skipping a beat in the conversation.

"All right, so embarrassing story. Oh, I know. You were asking if Oakley and I ever swapped places, so this one might tickle your fancy. Though it's not so much trading places as a mistaken identity."

"Oh no."

"There was this other pair of identical twins at the academy, and Oakley was determined for us to go on a double date with them, she read all those stories about identical twins who fell in love with identical twins and created near-identical children, and she just got it into her head that it would be romantic."

"Sounds more creepy than anything else."

"I don't disagree, but I love my sister and sometimes, it's easier to just go with it rather than doing anything else. Anyway, we went on this date, and she clicked with her twin, whereas I couldn't have been more indifferent about mine. We weren't a good fit for each other. We parted ways at the end of the night and no one seemed particularly bothered by it."

The server reappears with our wine. "Who would like to taste it?" he asks.

Clover and I exchange a panicked glance.

"Erm, I will." I move my glass closer to the edge of the table so the waiter can pour some into it. I pick up the glass and swill it around like I've seen other people do. I take a sip then nod because I think it's fine.

The server takes it as the sign to fill both of our glasses, then disappears.

"You have no idea what you were doing," Clover says.

"Not even slightly," I admit. "Did I at least look the part?"

"If the part was pretentious wine expert, then no."

I chuckle. "That's fair, but it tastes nice."

She picks up her glass and takes a sip. "It does."

"Your twin story?" I prompt.

"Right. So Oakley decided to keep dating the twin even though her fantasy of identical houses was ruined. He decided he wanted to surprise her with some cheesy indoor picnic. Only problem was, that he had no idea which room was hers, so he asked around by describing her, and whoever he asked told him to go to my room instead of hers."

"Oh no..."

"Yep, you can see where this is going right? So I've had a really hard day full of my least favourite subjects and I'm looking forward to just hanging out in my room and not having to worry about anything else, and I turn the key, open the door, and there's Oakley's date, completely naked except for a strategically placed baguette."

I burst out laughing, unable to help myself given the image she's describing. "A baguette?"

"Mmhmm."

"What did he think your sister was going to do with it?"

"I have no idea, because when I told her about it, she was mortified that he'd ever thought that was a good idea, not just because it was my room, but because it was a terrible idea for her too."

"I've not even met your sister and I feel sorry for her."

"Which is perhaps the true reason for my story," she jokes.

I smile at her, trying not to let myself get too lost in exactly how easy it is to talk to her. I never expected this when the witch opposite me walked into my office for the first time, but I have to admit that I find myself looking forward to seeing her every time.

Maybe that's something I need to stop fighting.

TEN

CLOVER

A BUSY DAY at the coffee shop is so different from a busy day at the bakery, though I can't put my finger on exactly why that is. Perhaps it's because I don't have to spend a busy day on my own in the same way. When it's like that at the bakery, the others come and go, torn between making up new things for the display cases, and helping me sell what we've got.

Here, Willow is always around. And on really busy days, Azíl or Ash are here too.

"Here you go," I say as I put down a takeaway

mocha in front of a wolf shifter. "Thanks for coming to Cauldron Coffee Shop."

She smiles at me and picks up her cup, heading towards the door.

I turn to serve the next customer, only to discover that there isn't one.

"Want a coffee?" Willow asks.

I nod. "I'd love a pumpkin spice latte."

"I know you would. Luckily, I learned to stock up on it long ago." She pulls two mugs down from their spot on top of the coffee machine and starts making them. "Will you pass me the milk?" she asks.

I hand it to her, and my sleeves roll up in the process. Willow's gaze flits to the new set of burns on my arms.

"Dare I ask?"

I sigh. "Tired and in charge of an oven aren't a good mix," I admit. "At least Rowen's good at soothing magic."

"You should ask Azíl about his healing spell, it works *so* much better than any of the ones they taught us."

"Huh, I didn't realise that."

"Neither did I until he used one on me. But I suppose what's the point of having an ancient boyfriend if he doesn't come with all of the perks of lost magic."

I snort. "Because *that's* the reason you're together."

"Oh yes, absolutely that. It's nothing to do with the fact he's smart, sweet, and handsome," she responds. "And has a nice accent."

"How far up the scale is that last one?"

She shrugs. "You can't tell me you don't appreciate a nice accent." She hands one of the lattes to me and takes the other one for herself.

"Hmm, maybe."

"All right, spill, what's on your mind?"

"How do you know there's anything?"

"Rowen's been teaching me big sister intuition," she quips. "Though really, I've known you for your entire life, I can tell when something's bothering you. And tired doesn't explain those burns. Those are lost in thought burns."

I snort. "You can't possibly know that."

"I burn myself more when I'm thinking about things than when I'm tired." She gives me a knowing look that suggests I'm not going to be able to pull the wool over her eyes on this one.

"I've just got so much on. I don't want to give any of it up."

"Don't you?" She takes a sip from her coffee. "Too hot, don't drink yet."

"I wasn't planning on it." I let out a loud sigh.

"We can cut your shifts back here," she says. "We'll hire someone."

"You don't want to hire anyone."

Willow grimaces. "I can't say I'm enamoured by the idea, but I also don't want you to be overworked, and that's clearly what's happening right now."

"I don't want to step back from the coffee shop," I admit. "I like it here, it feels like home. Do you know what I mean?"

"Considering I live here, I'm going to have to say yes. But I hate to point out that Sabine's old room is now Azíl's office, so you can't move in."

I let out a soft snort. "I love both you and Azíl dearly, but the idea of living with the two of you is awful. No offence."

She shrugs. "We're not that bad, but I see your point, I wouldn't want to live with a couple either."

"It's hard. I know I'm doing too much at the moment, but I just can't bring myself to drop anything. The bakery is so important to everyone, and I like it here, and there's my book..."

"Okay, so what is it about the book that's on your mind?"

I close my eyes and take a deep breath, knowing that she's the best person to talk to. "How do you manage a workplace romance?"

Surprise flits over her face. "I mean, I wouldn't really call it that. Azíl mostly worked here out of necessity at the beginning, especially before we broke his curse. Now he only does it when he needs a break from his proper work. Why? What's happened?"

"I like my editor."

"I think you're supposed to. At least when they're not telling you that what you've written is wrong."

"Oh that part's fine," I admit. "It's the part where we flirt but don't do anything about it that I'm struggling with. I asked him out for dinner the other night and we went to that restaurant that you and Azíl keep going on about. But I don't know if he knows I meant it as a date."

She raises an eyebrow. "How could he not know?"

I check there are no customers paying attention to us and pull out my phone, clicking through to my message chain with Tyler and show it to her.

"He knew," she says firmly.

"How can you tell?"

"You asked him out for dinner to a fancy restaurant and he replied straight away. Even if he didn't think it was a date, he definitely wanted to spend time with you, and doesn't that have the same effect?"

I frown. "Maybe."

"Look, you're both adults. If you want to know how he feels about the situation, then you need to ask him about it. Or at the very least, ask him on a date that leaves no room for interpretation."

"So you're saying that I should use the word date."

"Yes."

"What if it ruins the launch of my book?"

"Why would it?" The dishwasher beeps signalling that it's ended and she sets her mug down in order to deal with it.

"Because it might make things weird with my editor if he isn't interested in me."

Willow shrugs. "Then ask for a new one. He'd be an idiot to let it ruin the launch of your book though, especially when it's going to make them so much money."

"You don't know that."

"You said your advance is ten times what you expected, isn't that an indication of how well they think you're going to do?" Willow asks.

"I suppose. But I don't know enough about it to be sure."

"At least you'll know for the next one."

"You're very sure there's going to be another one."

"Because I know you. You're determined, smart, and good at what you do. It's not like this is your first foray into recipes, you've been doing it for a couple of years for the bakery's blog, and look how people respond to those."

"Why is everyone so good at being logical with me these days?" I mutter.

"Maybe because you're being slightly irrational."

"I'm not."

"Mmhmm."

I sigh. "I'm just tired and overthinking too much. Every time I consider what I want to take a step back on, I always come to the same conclusion, and I just don't know how to start the conversation."

"The bakery?"

I nod, knowing that I've mentioned the idea to her in passing before. Sometimes, it's easier to talk to Willow about these things because she doesn't have anything to do with the bakery itself, other than selling our cakes here. But she'd do that regardless.

"Okay, so if you choose to step back from the bakery, you have to remember that you're not abandoning it. You're still going to be working for it. Your cookbook will bring in a lot of interest, you might even be able to start a postal service. And maybe Rowen will be able to finally accept that she needs to hire some front-of-house staff so the five of you can focus on the things that matter. You've all been working on growing the business since just after she left the academy, surely it's about time that one of you switched to do something else?"

I blink a few times. "Have you thought about taking your own advice about the coffee shop?"

"I don't have any siblings to pick up the slack. Just a cousin who apparently likes it here, and Ash who just needs the money to finance whatever it is he does at Grimalkin."

I snort. "I'm pretty sure he just hangs out with Ellie most of the time."

"Fair enough. I'd probably do the same if I was in his position. Anyway, what I'm saying is that the others will understand if this is what you have to do. I know the bakery is important to you, but it's still your life and you have to do what makes you happy."

"You've grown very wise."

She snorts. "It's all the curse breaking."

"Didn't you only break one, and isn't it still an issue?"

"Yes, but I've done a lot of trying to fix it," she

jokes. "Whatever happens, Clo, you have a safe place here. I'm not going anywhere."

"Thanks, Willow."

"I mean it."

"I know you do." I smile at my cousin, pleased to know that I have her on my side even if that was something I was already aware of.

The bell rings, signalling the arrival of another customer, and I tear myself away from our conversation so I can take their order. I'm not sure what exactly I'm going to do about Tyler, or about the bakery, but I feel better for having said some of what I'm thinking out loud.

Now all I need is a little more clarity.

ELEVEN

TYLER

THE MOMENT I see Clover approaching the printing warehouse entrance, my heart skips a beat. She's not wearing anything particularly special, just jeans and a casual shirt, but she looks just as beautiful as she did the other night on our almost-date. I'm still not entirely sure whether she intended it that way, but considering how little we talked about work, I have to assume that's what it was.

"Hey," she says brightly as she sees me. She pauses, as if she wants to greet me in a different way, but thinks better of it before she can.

"Hi," I respond. "Are you ready for your tour?"

"I think so. I'm excited, I've never seen a book being printed."

"I fear that you're going to be disappointed, it's nothing like seeing an old printing press at work."

"Have you seen one to compare?"

"I've operated one," I respond. It was an experience day that I went on once, there were all kinds of old printing methods to try. It was a lot of fun." I smile at the memory.

"So you really are a book nerd."

"I'd prefer it to be known as a printing nerd," he responds. "I like books, but it's the process of making them that I really like. I've got several bookbinding qualifications too."

She raises an eyebrow. "Impressive. Though that provides at least some explanation about why you might not think that printing like this is interesting."

"I could take you to see a proper bookbinding in the future, if you want?"

"That depends."

"On?"

"Whether it's a date, or if it's just a professional courtesy thing." The way she looks at me makes it clear that the answer is important to her.

"I think I can think of better things to do on a date," I blurt out. "If you're interested in a date."

"Ah, so you didn't realise that's what the other

night was." A furious blush creeps over her cheeks. "I should have been clearer."

I reach out and touch her arm, unsure of exactly what I'm supposed to be doing right now. "I hoped that it was a date. But I was worried about what the answer was going to be, which is why I didn't ask."

"You should have done."

"I know." I clear my throat. "So how about I make it up to you by asking you on a date now."

"So long as you don't mean the tour of your printing warehouse," she jokes.

"I don't," I promise. "I was thinking about food. There's a great little Korean place in town if you like Korean food."

"I'm not sure I've ever had it," she responds. "But that sounds nice. Though I have to ask, is this place your house?"

I chuckle. "No."

"Is it bad that I'm a little bit disappointed?"

My heart skips a beat. "Not bad at all," I murmur.

"Good. We can keep that for another time. Now, what about this tour? I'm looking forward to seeing how it all works, even if you think it's not interesting compared to the proper process."

"I didn't say it wasn't interesting, just that I prefer the traditional methods."

"Sure, keep telling yourself that." She throws me what I think is a flirty smile, and actually, probably is.

Feeling brave, I place my hand on the small of her back and lead her inside the building. I know that I shouldn't be acting like this when we're in a work environment, but I can't help it, there's something about Clover that just makes me want to break all of the rules.

"You need to put some earplugs in," I say, gesturing towards the wall-mounted dispenser.

She nods and grabs a pair, sticking them in her ears.

I grab my own pair from around my neck, already regretting that it's going to be so loud in there and that we're not going to be able to talk as easily as we have been doing. That's the part of being around her that I like the most.

The loud whirr of the printing machines drowns out everything else, and the vibrations pass through me as we make our way onto the floor. Huge machines dominate the room, spewing out pages as quickly as they can.

"What are they printing?" Clover shouts over the noise.

"I'm not sure," I admit. "I didn't think to check the logs before I came in. The machines on this side of the room will be dealing with one book, while those at the other will be going on a different one."

"How come they don't get confused about what goes where?"

"Good question, I'm not sure. I think that they're working on books with different trim sizes, but sometimes accidents happen."

"Interesting." From the expression on her face, I actually believe that she means it too. She genuinely thinks that the process is intriguing.

I suppose it is. Most people haven't had a chance to see this first-hand, and considering that she isn't far off holding her own book in her hands, this probably means a lot more to her than it does to me. I've come out to the warehouse several times in the past year alone, which means that I know the ins and outs of it far better.

"When are you going to start printing my book?" she asks.

"In a couple of weeks, I think. We'll have the proof for you to approve soon."

"Do you always pay this much attention to your clients?"

"What do you mean?"

"I guess I'm surprised by how much of a say I get in things."

"We're not a big publisher," I respond. "Which

means that we can spend a bit more time working with our clients, rather than just telling them how it is."

"I have to say, I like the personal touch." She reaches out and places a hand on my arm.

I smile at her, hoping she realises the effect she's having on me.

In all likelihood, she absolutely does. Or she doesn't, but I'm having a similar one on her. Which I'm not about to complain about, especially when it means that the two of us are going to share a date where we're both completely aware that it's a date.

I don't think I've ever been so excited at the prospect of simply eating before, but when the company is this good, there's every reason to be looking forward to it.

TWELVE

Clover

THE RESTAURANT'S atmosphere is so unlike the one I chose the other day, and it makes me feel as if he's brought me to somewhere a lot more intimate despite the fact that the lighting is quite bright and there are no candles on the table.

"I should have asked if you know how to use chopsticks," he says as the various dishes he's ordered for us start to arrive.

"I do," I assure him. "I'm not great at them, but I'm passable." Certainly enough that I'm not about to make a fool out of myself using them.

"I have to admit I'm relieved. I think they might have forks if we ask them for some..."

"It's fine," I assure him. "I don't need a fork, I'm good with these. And there's a spoon in the rice if I get really stuck." I gesture to it.

"Hmm, true."

"So where do we start?" I ask, scanning the delicious-smelling food in front of me and trying to decide what to eat first.

"Anything. The idea is that you eat a bit of everything but in whatever order you want."

"All right, then I'll try this a different way. Which is your favourite?"

"The chicken wings." He picks up the plate and holds them out to me.

"An interesting choice for a first date," I respond.

"You said that our dinner the other night was a date," he points out. "Which makes this our second."

"I'd argue with you, but I like the idea of this being our second date too much." I reach out and pick up one of the chicken wings with my fingers. If he's going to be put off with me eating it like this, then perhaps it's better if we don't have a third date.

Then again, Tyler is the one who suggested the restaurant, which means that he knew this was what was going to happen.

I bite into the chicken and let out a small hum of appreciation. "That's delicious."

"I know," he responds. "Here, try some of this." He puts a small bowl of red cabbage-like stuff down in front of me.

"What is it?"

"Kimchi," he responds. "It's fermented."

Intrigued, I pick up my chopsticks and lift some to my mouth so I can taste it. "Mmm, it's spicy."

"Sorry, I should have checked you were okay with that."

"I am." And I'm going to have to tell Willow about this place, Azíl will love it. "Have you been to Korea?" I ask him after a few more bites of food.

He nods. "I haven't been in years, but I went a lot when I was younger."

"What's it like?"

"Beautiful in places, crowded in others," he responds. "Have you been?"

"No, I haven't really travelled much. Just the normal places."

"What's normal to you?"

"France, mostly. Though I've been to Spain a few times. My aunt and uncle have a house over there that they let us use sometimes."

"Would you want to travel more?"

"I'd love to, there's just never really been time

for it," I admit. "I've always been busy with the bakery or with studying. I've been on a few girls' weekends with my friends from the academy, but you know what those are like."

He chuckles. "Unsurprisingly, I don't know what a girls' weekend is like."

"Oh, it's mostly drinking and hanging out by the pool while we catch up." I eat some more of the food, impressed with the amount of flavour that's packed into every bite.

"That sounds like a good kind of holiday," he responds.

"Oh, don't get me wrong, it's great fun, and always good because we need lots of time to catch up on one another's lives. But it's not the kind of travelling I want to do. Ideally, I'd want to spend a lot more time looking at the places of historical significance, and trying all of the local food. Maybe learning how witches used to live there. You know, that kind of thing."

"That does sound good," he admits. "I've only really had that experience in Korea, but it was fun. It would be nice to do it elsewhere."

"If life allowed for it." I sigh and take a sip of water.

"Yeah, that's the real problem, isn't it?"

"That and finding someone who wants to go with

me. I suppose I could go on my own, but it's just not the same as discovering something with someone, know what I mean?"

He nods. "Some things are meant to be shared."

"Exactly. This is really good food, by the way."

"Wait until I cook for you then, if you think this is good, mine's better."

I raise an eyebrow. "Those are bold words, and not just because this is *really* good. You're assuming I'm going to let you cook for me." I nudge him gently so he knows that I'm only jesting.

"I'm making an educated guess based on how much I'm enjoying my time with you."

"Now that's a smooth line, how long have you been practising that one for?"

He chuckles deeply. "Only a couple of minutes."

"Then I just have to assume that you're a smooth talker. I should guard myself against that."

"Or you could let yourself fall for my charms," he responds.

"It might be too late for that." I'm suddenly very aware of how close the two of us are sitting, and the fact that we're leaning towards one another. If I move ever so slightly, we could kiss.

I clear my throat and sit back. Not because I don't want to do that, but because this isn't the right time or place to share our first.

"So, what are desserts like here?" I ask.

"They're good, but not as good as the savoury food," he responds. "Why?"

"Because I happen to have some delicious cake back at my flat," I say slowly, feeling bolder than I have in a while. "I thought perhaps we could go there for dessert. I have some fancy coffee that Willow gave me too."

"I'm confused if you're actually offering me coffee and cake, or if you're just trying to invite me back to your flat for something else."

I let out a bemused laugh. "I'm genuinely offering you coffee and cake," I respond. "But I wouldn't rule out the rest."

"That's a very tempting offer." He searches my face, as if he's trying to work out whether I'm serious about it or not.

"Are you going to take me up on it?" My heart pounds as I wait for him to respond. As much as I want to pretend I don't care if he says yes, I do. It's not that I want to rush anything, more that I don't want the night to end. I don't think I can ever get enough of his company.

"Yes."

I beam.

"But only if you're sure," he says quickly.

"More than sure." I use my chopsticks to pinch

one of the pickles from in front of him. "But I also want to spend my time finishing this delicious food too. I don't want to waste it, though I'm getting really full."

"We can ask for them to box it up for us, you can have it for lunch tomorrow."

"Hmm, that does sound good."

"Then let's do that and go get some coffee."

"You just want to see my flat, don't you?" I joke.

"You're the one who invited me to see it."

"Hmm, true. All right, you've twisted my arm."

He chuckles and catches the attention of the server, while I enjoy the way this is turning out. Good food, good company, and several more hours of it ahead. That's the perfect date in my mind, it's hard to believe that I'm actually on it.

THIRTEEN

CLOVER

I BRING the steaming cafetière into the living room
and set it down on the low table in front of my sofa.
"It'll be ready in a couple of minutes," I say.

"You weren't joking when you said you had
fancy coffee."

"It's a perk of doing some shifts for my cousin,
she gives me the first pick of all of the fancy coffees
that she gets delivered."

"And she knows her stuff?"

"When it comes to coffee, certainly." I sit down
next to him on the sofa.

"So, you've got a cousin for coffee, what's your

excuse for the cakes? You just happen to have all of these hanging around in your house?" He gestures to the plate which has half a dozen of the bakery's finest pieces on it.

I chuckle. "They're actually taste testers. I'm going to the coffee shop in the morning and these are for my cousin's boyfriend. He's started trying all of our cakes before they go on sale."

"Won't he mind that we've eaten them?"

"I hope not. But if he does, I'll just bribe him with more of them."

"Ah, using cake to get what you want, I see."

I let out a soft snort. "It's my superpower."

"And here I was thinking that was flirting."

"Only if yours is smooth-talking, you always seem to know what to say."

"Trust me, I really don't," Tyler responds. "It's only with you that I seem to have developed a knack for it."

I raise an eyebrow. "So does that mean that I'm a good influence on you, or a bad one?"

"The jury is out." Amusement is written all over his face. "So what cakes have you got for us?"

"I think this one is our best bet," I say, picking up one of Oakley's cupcakes. "Oak is calling it first-date glow. She was trying to get it ready for

Valentine's Day, but she couldn't get the recipe right."

"Interesting, but there's something I want to do before we eat that," he responds.

"Oh?"

He takes the cupcake from me and places it back on the table. He turns back to me and reaches out, cupping my cheek in his hand. My breathing hitches as understanding over what's about to happen comes over me. Perhaps we should have done this before I invited him up to my flat, but I find that I don't care. We seem to have been doing all kinds of things out of order, and this is just one of them.

Tyler leans forward and my eyes flutter closed. The anticipation grows inside me, only stopping the build when his lips brush against mine.

I kiss him back instantly, wrapping my arms around his neck and leaning even closer. His hand rests on the small of my back, while the other tangles in my hair.

Nothing matters other than the way it feels to kiss him. Everything is about the way it feels to have his lips against mine and to feel his body this close.

We break apart and I find myself smiling widely.

"Now I'm ready for the cupcake," he says. "I want to see how it feels compared to that."

"It's not as good," I murmur.

He shoots me a knowing smile, as if he's certain that I'm right. "Want some?" He holds the cupcake out to me.

I swipe my finger through the frosting and eat it straight from my finger, enjoying the way he watches me even if I know I'm being a little cruel with what I'm doing.

He raises an eyebrow. "You're a tease, you know that?"

"I don't believe that's the right word for it," I respond. "Especially when you're currently in my flat after a date."

"Hmm, true." He takes a bite of the cupcake and makes an appreciative noise. "It's delicious, but not better than our kiss."

I let out a bemused laugh. "I'd hope not. This isn't supposed to be the real emotion, only give you a shot that *feels* like it."

"Like the banana sweets that don't taste like bananas?"

"Except that they do. They use an artificial version of banana flavour that's derived from a species that no longer exists. So it feels like it out bananas the real thing, but actually, you're just tasting an extinct variant."

"None of that changes the fact that banana-flavoured stuff tastes bad," he points out.

"Unless it's banoffee pie, though I suppose you could argue that's not banana flavoured, it's just bananas."

"Does anyone really like banoffee pie, though?" he asks.

"You're about to find out, that's this one." I pick up the pie. "Hazel's been dying for us to sell a banoffee pie for years, but Rowen kept saying no until Hazel promised that she'd make it fancy. This is what she's come up with."

"What's the emotion?"

"See if you can guess?" I hold the pie out for him and he leans forward to take a bite. There's something intimate about the moment, even though all we're doing is eating some cakes and talking about them.

"Oh, that feels like comfort. Is that an emotion?"

"Maybe it's more of a feeling than an emotion, but it definitely evokes it, right?"

He nods. "I like it, even if banoffee pie isn't my favourite."

I take a bite myself and chew on it, enjoying the flavours despite it not being mine either. I set it down on the platter and turn back to Tyler.

"You have cream on your nose," he says, leaning in to wipe it away.

"Is this an excuse for you to get close to me again?" I ask.

"It's a situation I'm planning on taking advantage of," he responds, leaning in and kissing me again. His lips taste of the caramel topping of the pie making it all the sweeter.

At this rate, the coffee and the rest of our cake is going to end up completely forgotten, as I feel as if I may very well end up completely lost in him.

It's not something that I feel bad about. If anything, I welcome it with open arms. The only question is whether I'm going to be strong enough to send him home.

And whether I have to.

FOURTEEN

Clover

"Come in," Tyler calls the moment I knock on his door. I push it open and step inside, all of my worries about the reception I'm going to get disappearing the moment I see his face light up. "Hey."

"Hi."

"You're early."

"Barely." I make my way over to his desk, while he gets to his feet and comes around to the other side of the desk.

He leans in and presses a swift kiss against my lips despite the fact we're at his place of work. It sends small flutters through me that he doesn't care about that. Or maybe he does care, and this is just his way of showing exactly how much he cares about me and how seriously he's taking whatever it is growing between us.

Which shouldn't be much of a surprise considering the numerous dates we've been on over the past couple of weeks.

"I brought you some baklava," I say, holding out the box to him. "And a strawberry tart for your dad."

"He's going to think you're trying to bribe him."

"Better get it in before I'm trying to get his approval as your girlfriend too, then," I say without thinking about it. "I'm sorry, I shouldn't have said that."

"It's fine, Clover," he says. "I'd like it if you were my girlfriend."

"Are you sure?"

"Why would I say it if I wasn't?"

"I don't know, maybe you don't want me to make a run for it and ruin the launch of the cookbook."

"Trust me, that's the last thing on my mind when it comes to our relationship."

I beam widely at him.

"But this does mean that you're going to have to come to a family dinner at my house soon."

"You want me to meet your family?"

"It'll help put a stop to them trying to set me up with people, so really, it's a favour you're doing me," he jokes.

I shake my head in bemusement. "Then I'd be honoured. But you'll need to tell me what cakes I can bring, then at least I can make a good impression on your mum."

"You'll make a good impression anyway," he promises.

"Mmhmm, I'm not sure whether I believe you."

"You should."

"Okay, well all of that aside, I assume you didn't invite me to your office in order to talk about family dinner. What did you need to see me for?"

"You make it sound so mercenary," Tyler jokes. "But you're right, I actually asked you here so that you could do some final approvals before we send the cookbook to print."

"Oh, I didn't realise that was so soon." Nerves of a different kind flutter in my stomach as I consider what this means.

"It's not quite finished," he says. "But take a look." He gestures to his desk where a hardback book sits.

I take a deep breath, trying to quell the nerves within me. I set the box of pastries down on his desk and pull the book towards me, staring at the cover. The Broomstick Bakery logo is at the bottom of the cover along with my name. The binding is a light blue that matches our logo, a nice touch that shows Tyler's attention to detail.

"This is really it?" I ask, my voice barely coming out as barely a whisper as I run my hand over the cover.

"Yes."

"It doesn't seem real," I admit, realising that I can tell him these things now that he's more than just my editor.

"Why don't you open it?"

I nod and slowly open the front cover. The introduction I wrote looks beautiful next to photos from the bakery of us going about our day-to-day activities. Or that's what it looks like. In reality, they're all completely staged, but I know that's just how it has to be.

I slowly turn through the pages, seeing each of my recipes professionally laid out and photographed. My siblings had some input into them, mostly with corrections when I haven't gotten the method quite right, but this is my work. The thing that I've put months of late nights into.

A tear rolls down my face and splashes against the page, taking me by surprise.

Tyler reaches out and places a comforting hand on the small of my back, the gesture so small and familiar that it opens the floodgates all the more.

For a moment, I think he's going to get uncomfortable and not want to deal with me. Instead, he turns me and pulls me close, putting his arms around me and rubbing my back without saying a word. It's an intimate moment, one that I'm going to remember for the rest of my life.

"I'm sorry," I murmur into his chest. "I don't know what's wrong with me."

"Nothing is wrong with you," he says in a low and reassuring tone. "This is something you've worked really hard for, you're bound to feel at least a little emotional."

"I wouldn't call this a little." I wipe away my tears hastily, not wanting to scare him off when we've just shared a serious moment with one another.

"I promise, I understand how you feel," he says. He leans over his desk and pulls out a couple of tissues, handing them to me so I can wipe my face.

"I didn't expect to feel like this," I admit. "It's just a cookbook."

"But it's not." His tone is calm and reassuring,

making me wonder whether this isn't the first time he's had a conversation like this with someone. "This is your hard work. Not just the writing of it, but learning your craft at the bakery, and building your business. It's your passion and determination that have made this happen."

"And your hard work."

"Sure, I've put a lot into the organisation of the physical product, but I haven't written the words on the page, simply suggested a few tweaks."

I nod. "Thank you, even if it was just logistics that you did."

He chuckles. "I have a lot more logistics to do still. We need to organise a launch party, and get all of the other things sorted. Some signings, appearances, advertising that you've got the book coming. Do you already have access to the Broomstick Bakery website and social media?"

I nod.

"Okay, well that's one less thing to organise. I'll have the marketing department prepare all of those materials for you," he says. "As for the launch party, we might be able to pull in a favour with Chef DeRosssi if you want to hold it at the cookery school. If his son is dating your sister, it's probably possible. It's unfortunate that the bakery is too small and doesn't have a customer area."

"It doesn't," I say slowly. "But my cousin's coffee shop does. And she already sells our cakes."

"It has some advantages, especially with the built-in ability to serve drinks," he muses. "Do you think she'd be okay with that?"

"I imagine so, I'd have to ask." But even as I say it, I know there isn't a single chance that Willow will say no. She'll probably be pleased that she gets an excuse to celebrate me like that.

"Then we can work with that as our idea for it. But first we need to go through the book and make sure that everything is exactly the way you want it. There are some things we can't change, but I'll walk you through those."

"Thank you. For all of this. I know you're not doing it as a favour to me, and that the business is set to make some good money off the launch, but I still want you to know that I'm grateful. I know you've gone above and beyond for me."

He chuckles. "I've just done my job. Though to be clear, dating you is definitely *not* part of my job description, I've been doing that on my own time."

"Good to know. Though I hope that doesn't mean you have a no-making-out-in-the-office rule?" I look up at him in time to see amusement dance over his features.

"Believe it or not, there's no such rule in place."

"That's a shame, breaking that rule would have been fun."

"Maybe, but without one, I can do this all I want." He leans in and presses his lips against mine. The kiss is tender, as if he's using it to give me comfort and reassurance, both in his emotions, and in the situation we've found ourselves in.

I can't say that I ever expected my cookbook journey to end like this. Though I suppose this isn't actually the end, more like the middle of things. But it makes me excited for what's to come next.

CLOVER

I WRING my hands together and try not to think too much about the conversation that's to come. Especially as I know that now is the time to have it. Maybe I should have taken Willow up on her offer of talking to Rowen with me, but I turned her down, knowing that it's important for me to do this on my own.

"Row? Can I talk to you?" My voice shakes and I know there's nothing I can do to stop it. I'm not going to be able to relax until this conversation is over.

My older sister looks up from her seat at the

kitchen table, a concerned expression on her face. "You okay?"

I sigh and take a seat. "Maybe?"

"Not a particularly reassuring answer," she responds. "What's up?"

I swallow my nerves and try to avoid fiddling with my shirt, though I'm finding it hard to. "I want to step back from the baking side of the bakery," I blurt.

Surprise flits across Rowen's face.

"I've been thinking about it a lot," I say before she can respond with anything that might be an attempt to talk me out of it.

"Okay."

I blink a few times. "Okay?"

"What would you prefer I said?"

"I don't know, I guess I just thought that you'd do everything you could to talk me out of it."

"Well for one, you haven't said anything I can argue with," she points out. "And you're also an adult who can make your own mind up about things."

"I guess it just feels weird for me to admit that out loud. Well, to you. I've said it out loud before."

"To Willow?"

It's my turn to be surprised.

"I know that you two are close," she says, and it

makes sense that you wouldn't go to Hazel or Oakley about this."

I sigh. "I've been struggling for a while," I admit. "No one seems to want my baklava as much as they want the other stuff here, and I'm always relegated to the front, and it's just been making me really unhappy. I just didn't realise until I started helping Willow at the coffee shop last year, that feels so different."

Rowen leans back in her seat and nods.

"I know that it's probably not ideal, and I'll obviously take a pay cut from the bakery income, but that should at least make it easier to squeeze in the money to pay Ash when he joins the bakery properly, right?" I know that it's a little sneaky to use that as my reasoning, but at least it benefits my sisters and brother.

"I hadn't thought of that," Rowen says. "Are you stepping back from the coffee shop too?"

I let out a sigh of relief at her question. If she's asking it like that, then she must not be as opposed to the idea as I thought she might be. "I don't think so. I actually thought that I could just make my baklava there instead. That way we can still sell it at the coffee shop and we don't lose that income."

Rowen nods. "Is Willow okay with that?"

"I assume so. She's offered me use of her kitchen

in the past, so I assume the offer will still stand."

"Good. Then I guess that's all there is to it."

"You're not going to try and talk me out of it?"

"Why would I? After Ash asked me about joining the bakery, I started paying more attention to what's going on with you all, and I realised you weren't particularly happy with the way things were. You've only seemed to perk up since starting your cookbook."

I smile. "Yeah, that's been a lot of fun. And it's still part of the bakery. I don't want to leave, I just want to do other things."

My older sister nods. "Are you sure you want to take a pay cut if you're still going to be part of it?"

"Yes. I'll have the royalties from my book," I point out. "Well, the royalties that I don't pay into the bakery funds."

She raises an eyebrow. "I didn't realise you were planning on doing that."

"I kind of have to, Row. Without the bakery's reputation, or the expertise you all have and shared with me, there wouldn't be a book. So I need to share what I make with you."

"Okay. But we'll earmark it for marketing instead of paying it into any of our pockets."

"That sounds good," I agree, relieved that she isn't going to try and fight me on this. I've thought about it long and hard while the money from my advance sits in my account and stares at me.

"I guess we'll have to start job interviews for some front-of-house staff," Rowen says. "Especially with the lot of you convincing me to go to the Staffordshire show."

"I think you should go to more than just that one," I respond. "It'll be good for the bakery."

"You guys are going to have to stop using that logic to get me to do what you want," she half-jokes.

"Why would we when it works?" I reach across the table and give her hand a squeeze. "But this is a good thing, Row. We're expanding. Isn't that what you want?"

Indecision wars over her face. "I don't know."

"Yeah, you do, you've just been scared to admit it."

"You're my little sister, you're not supposed to understand these things."

"I'm not so little any more," I remind her. "And we've all been working hard. Oakley's wedding cake orders are up from last year, Hazel working with DeRossi's son is going to bring some attention to us. It hasn't happened yet. Can you imagine what will happen if we end up supplying the cakes at one of his events?"

"Mmm, and that's without your cookbook."

"We don't know how that's going to go," I point out. "It could be a flop."

"But your editor is confident it's going to go well, right?"

I nod.

"And the owner of the publishing house?"

"I think so, though I haven't met him yet."

Surprise flits across her face. "You haven't?"

"No. But I will on Friday night."

"Shouldn't you be meeting him during business hours?"

A furious blush rushes to my cheeks. "Erm, it's more like a family dinner situation," I murmur. "Tyler's taking me with him."

She narrows her eyes at me. "That's a very familiar thing for him to do for a client."

"I'm not going as a client," I admit.

"You move fast."

"It's been a month," I point out. "Maybe a bit longer. And that's more time than it took for you to introduce Edward to Mum and Dad."

"That's different," she mumbles.

"Is it? Because from where I'm standing, it looks like the only difference is that you're the one involved in one of those situations, and I'm the one in the other."

"I'm not working with Edward though, there's

the difference."

"You didn't have an issue with it when Hazel and Antonio started dating, and she didn't even realise who she was going out with. At least I know."

Rowen lets out a snort of amusement. "All right, that's a fair point. I just don't want to see you get hurt."

"I don't particularly want to get hurt either," I point out. "But I know that ignoring the way I feel when I'm around Tyler isn't going to help that. Besides, this is your fault. It was your advice that made me message him for dinner in the first place. You can't go back on that now."

"You've got me there," she responds. "I just hope you know what you're doing."

"No more than anyone else does," I point out.

"True."

The door bursts open and we both turn our attention in that direction in time to see Oakley bursting in with a huge smile on her face.

"You're here," she says, bouncing over to us both.

"Everything okay, Oak?" I ask, trying to avoid giving any hint to her that I know what could have put her in this kind of mood.

"Justin proposed!" She holds out her hand so we

can see the ring.

"It's beautiful," Rowen says.

"Congrats." My lips ache from the wide smile on my face.

She narrows her eyes. "You knew."

I let out a small laugh. "I did, yes."

She sits down next to me and leans her head against my shoulder. "You'll be my maid of honour, right?"

"You know I will, Oak. What are twins for?"

"Exactly what I thought." She lets out a dreamy smile and stares at her ring. "People aren't going to say it's too soon, are they?"

"Let them," Rowen responds. "Their opinion doesn't matter, the only people who get a say in this are you and Justin, and if you're ready, then you're ready."

I raise an eyebrow at my older sister.

She lets out a resigned groan. "Fine, I admit it, I'm a secret romantic."

"Not so secret any more," I tease.

She smiles, but I can tell that most of her attention is on my twin sister. Which is exactly where it should be in this situation. It's exciting to think that my sister is getting married, but I know that it's the right thing for her, and that she and Justin are going to have a very happy marriage.

SIXTEEN

TYLER

I OPEN the car door for Clover, noticing the nerves written all over her face. I reach out and place my hand on her lower back. She leans into my touch, which reassures me that she wants to be here, she's just feeling a little uncertain about what's to come.

I don't blame her, I'm sure I'll feel exactly the same when it's time for her to introduce me to her family properly. I've met some of her sisters in passing, but it's not the same as being properly introduced as her boyfriend.

"Are you ready?" I ask her.

"Just let me grab the cakes."

I nod and wait for her to retrieve the boxes she put on the back seat of the car when she got in. It's hard to believe how many she's brought, but I know that's a little on me for telling her that Mum loves the bakery's bakes.

"Okay, I'm ready. I think. Maybe I should have met your dad at the office first." She glances up at the house as if trying to get a sense of the people who live inside. Not that it would help much, it's just a normal building on a street of houses that look basically the same.

"Do you want me to carry anything?" I ask.

She shakes her head. "Let me focus on the boxes."

"Okay." I know better than to argue with her about this. Instead, I open the gate and lead her up to the front door. I'm not as nervous as I thought I'd be about introducing a girlfriend to my parents. It's been a long time since I've done anything like this, but I know they're going to like her, which makes it a lot easier.

I press the doorbell, then open the door anyway, getting a strange look from Clover.

"I'm coming!" Mum calls through the house.

"It's me," I call back.

She shuffles into the hallway, her favourite apron still pristine despite the fact I know she'll have been cooking for the past few hours.

"Tyler, honey." She heads in my direction and pulls me into a hug.

"Hi, Mum."

"You're looking well."

"You know I am, you saw me last week," I remind her.

"Your dad said that you've brought a guest this week."

"I have. Mum, this is my girlfriend, Clover," I say, gesturing back to the brunette witch.

Clover steps forward. "It's nice to meet you, Mrs Kim."

"Oh, she's a polite one. Where did you find her?" Mum asks.

I chuckle. "Clover is the author I've been working on."

"I thought you were working on the Broomstick Bakery cookbook?"

"I have."

Mum looks past me and squints at Clover. "I thought you seemed familiar."

"I'm Clover Parkes," she says. "My family owns the bakery."

"Oh, gosh, well you should come straight in, I love your cakes."

"Tyler said that the gingerbread biscuits that

we make at Christmas are your favourites," she says.

Mum's face lights up. "I love them."

"I asked my sister to make you a batch," Clover says. "They're in the bottom box, I think. And then there's some strawberry tarts for Mr Kim, and a cake for dessert. If you want it. You can save it for another time if you want."

Ah, so that's why she brought so many boxes, it makes sense now.

"You're such a sweetheart," Mum says. "Well come in, come in, you shouldn't be standing in the doorway. Your sister is here already."

"Oh good, I meant to talk to her about..."

"No work talk," Mum says. "You know my rules about those things. I'm sure you understand, dear," she says to Clover.

"My parents have the same rule," she responds. "They hate it when we all start talking about work stuff."

"For good reason, there's a place for that, and it's in the office," Mum says. "Tyler, why don't you bring the cakes to the kitchen." She gives me a stern look that I know I have to listen to, or I'll get a stern talking-to later.

I turn to Clover who hands them over to me, no doubt realising that there's no arguing. "The living room is through those doors, I'll be back in a moment."

She nods and touches my hand gently. I can tell from her expression that she wants to show me more affection, but doesn't dare to.

I follow Mum into the kitchen and set the boxes on the counter. I take a peek into each of them and put the box with the strawberry tarts in the fridge.

"A girlfriend, Tyler?" Mum asks in Korean. "And here I was thinking that you were going to be single for the rest of your days."

"That's a little dramatic, don't you think?" I respond in the same language.

"You've refused to be set up with any of the suggestions your dad and I have suggested."

"That's because I didn't want my parents to set me up with anyone, which I keep telling you."

"Don't be so cheeky." She flashes me a stern look. "But she seems nice."

"I'm glad you like her."

"I wouldn't go that far, I barely know her, but she brought cake."

"Your favourites," I point out. "I didn't know she was going to do that."

"Hmm. Now take through the tray of drinks," Mum says, gesturing to the tray on the kitchen side.

"Got it." I lean in and kiss her cheek before

grabbing the tray and taking it through to the living room where Dad and Joyce are sitting with Clover.

I flash a reassuring smile in her direction and place the tray down on the counter.

"Clover was just telling us about your tour of the book-binding facility," Dad says.

"I thought it would help if she saw how these things work," I respond after a moment of trying to work out which language I should be using. Normally when it's just my family around, we speak Korean, but that's not right when Clover is in the room.

"It was very impressive," Clover says as she accepts a glass from me. "I've never seen anything like it."

Dad chuckles. "I imagine I'd say the same if I was in your kitchen. I can't say I'd be of much use there."

"We could always find a good use for you, Mr Kim, even if it's washing dishes."

He lets out a booming laugh. "I like her, son."

"I'm glad." I sit down next to Clover and put my arm around her.

"Though I can't say this is what I expected when I gave you the account to look after," Dad says.

"It wasn't what I expected from my first meeting with your son either," Clover says, placing a gentle hand on my knee and giving it a squeeze so I know she's okay.

"Did you know that Clover's sister is dating DeRossis's son?" I ask Dad.

He raises an eyebrow. "It's a small world."

"Certainly within the culinary circuit," Clover responds.

"I wasn't aware DeRossi Junior was seeing anyone," Joyce puts in.

"Disappointed that you can't date him yourself?" I tease.

"If you'd tasted his cooking, you'd know why. The man is a genius when it comes to sauces," she responds. "Though I know he doesn't do much savoury work."

"He's planning on changing that," Clover says. "He was talking about it over dinner at Christmas. He's hoping to open his own restaurant at some point."

Dad raises an eyebrow. "Then perhaps we'll end up with another cookbook to add to our roster. I think we could make a name for ourselves in witch and warlock cooking."

"I suppose we're probably well cut out for it thanks to the potion-making," Clover says.

"You might be onto something there," Dad says.

The door opens and Mum comes into the room.

"You'd better not be talking about work in here," she says, eyeing up the four of us.

"Absolutely not, my dear," Dad says, getting to his feet. "Do you need to have any help?"

"No, everything is all set up in the dining room, you can go through now," she says, gesturing to the double doors that lead through there.

Joyce gets to her feet and follows Mum the moment she heads back to the kitchen, knowing that she'll be needed to take things through.

Dad heads straight off to the dining room, mostly because he wants to steal some of the pickles that Mum will already have put there.

"Are you okay?" I ask Clover.

She nods. "Your family are lovely."

"Even if they're giving you the tenth degree?"

She smiles at me reassuringly. "I promise it's fine. You'll fare much worse with my family."

"You know what? I'm looking forward to it."

"I'm glad." she leans in and presses a kiss against my cheek. "Now I'm starving, and really looking forward to your Mum's cooking, you've made it sound delicious."

"You should say that in front of her, she'll love you forever."

"I'm not sure she's quite there yet," Clover points out. "Though the cake seemed to help."

"Mmm, I think she's pleased with that, even if she'd not saying as much."

"Then I'm going to do everything I can to make sure I'm giving the best impression I can."

"You don't need to try," I assure her. "You'll manage that just by being yourself. You did with me."

"Ah, but mums are completely different creatures, I need to work at least twice as hard to impress her as I did you."

"I'm not sure if I should be insulted or not."

"Not even slightly," she responds. "It just means that I care about you a lot."

"The feeling is entirely mutual."

The way she looks at me makes me certain that she means every word, and that this is going to be something that lasts for a long time to come.

SEVENTEEN

Clover

I THREAD through the crowd mostly made up of Oakley's friends and find my way to the table at the back where I left Tyler with Hazel and Antonio. At least the two men know one another in passing, so it's not too difficult for them to find things to talk about.

"Hey," I say, sitting down next to Tyler and handing him the drink I brought.

His face lights up. "You're back."

"I am. I told you I was only going to get us drinks," I remind him, setting my own down on the table.

He chuckles. "Yes, but there was always going to be a chance that you got lost on your way back."

"We're in my twin sister's house."

"With loads of people you know and probably haven't seen in ages."

"He's got a point," Hazel agrees.

I roll my eyes. "Maybe I just thought it was better if I was waiting with you when Mum and Dad arrive."

Hazel chuckles. "Shouldn't they be here by now? I'm surprised they're late to Oakley's engagement party."

I shrug. "You know what Mum's like, she probably forgot the card and made Dad turn around to get it."

The doorbell rings.

"Ah, there we go, that's going to be them," I say.

"We must have said their names too many times," Hazel quips.

I chuckle and get to my feet, holding my hand out to Tyler. "Ready?"

He nods, though I can tell he's nervous.

"If I managed with just your sister there, you can manage with all kinds of people."

"I know that, I just want to make a good impression," Tyler responds.

"You will." I go up on my toes and kiss his cheek. "They're going to love you."

"You don't know that for sure."

"I do, because I love you." The words slip out without me meaning them to, though it's not the first time that's nearly happened. I've been tempted to tell him more than once already but the timing hasn't felt right.

His face softens and he turns to me, brushing his fingers against my cheek. "I love you too, Clover." He leans in and captures my lips with his, completely oblivious to all of the people around us. But I don't care, the only thing that matters is the way he's making me feel.

We pull apart, both of us grinning widely.

"Now I'm ready to meet your parents," he murmurs.

"Okay, come on then." I slip my hand into his and draw him towards the front door where Mum and Dad are already saying hello to my sisters and their partners. I don't know where Ash and his girlfriend have gotten to, but they're around here somewhere.

"Good to see you again, Antonio," Dad says, clapping him on the back in greeting.

"Hi, Mum," I say, pulling her into a hug as she reaches us.

"Clover, sweetie, it's been a while since you've come for dinner," she says, pulling back and looking me up and down before giving an approving nod. She must think that I'm looking well enough not to comment on it. "And who is this?"

"This is Tyler."

"Ah, yes, the boyfriend," Dad says as he comes to join us. "I've been hearing about you." He holds out his hand for Tyler to shake.

"It's good to meet you, Mr Parkes."

Dad chuckles. "There's no need for all of that, you can call me Barry."

Tyler smiles. "I appreciate it."

"You'll have to come over for dinner," Mum says. "What about two weeks on Thursday?"

"I can't, Mum, that's my book launch party. You're supposed to be coming to it."

"Oh, right, silly me, I forgot about that. Is your publisher coming?"

"Tyler is my publisher. Sort of." I smile at him reassuringly. "His dad owns the publishing company, it's how we met."

Surprise flits over her face. "Rowen failed to mention that when she came for dinner." She shoots a disapproving look at my older sister who grimaces and mouths the word sorry in my direction.

I simply smile. I know what Mum's like. No doubt she was trying to avoid having to answer too many questions that she didn't know the answer to. Or saving me from a call that ended up with me being told off. Whatever the reason, I'm grateful to Rowen for it.

"I see we're going to have a lot to catch up on," Mum says.

"But it's Oakley and Justin's night," I remind her. "We're here to celebrate them."

"We are. Is your brother here yet?"

"He's somewhere around with Ellie," I respond.

"All right, I'll do my rounds and try to find him," she says. "Come on, Barry."

Dad gives me a reassuring smile and follows her into the crowd.

"See, that wasn't so bad," I say to Tyler.

He chuckles. "It wasn't."

"It was better than when Oakley introduced them to Justin, do you remember?" Hazel asks.

I laugh. "Oh yeah, they asked him all kinds of questions about how they met and why he'd been so forgiving after Oak nearly ruined his sister's wedding."

"Which was a bit of a stretch when all she really did was make a mistake with the cupcakes that she fixed," Hazel responds. "And then there was the reaction when Rowen introduced them to Edward at the Christmas meal."

I snort.

"Dare I ask?" Tyler looks between us, almost as if trying to decide if he wants to hear the story.

"I think Mum was more surprised that Rowen had brought someone with her than anything else, while all Dad did was chunter about how he hadn't bought enough beer," Hazel says. "As if he's ever underbought it."

"Especially when Edward brought that delicious wine from his vineyard," I respond. "We should ask him for a bottle to take to your parents," I say to Tyler.

"He owns a vineyard?"

"His brother runs it, Edward himself is a lawyer of some kind, you'll have to ask him about it."

"Knowing my luck, he'll have been at the same law school as Joyce and will be totally put off me already," Tyler mutters.

"Which makes it sound like I need to have a conversation with your sister about what you used to be like," I tease.

"Please don't, I dread to think of the horror stories she'll tell."

"And I want to hear them all," I respond. "I want to know everything about you."

"Hopefully none of it will be about to send you running for the hills," he jokes.

I turn and wrap my arms around his neck. "I'm almost certain that it won't."

He raises an eyebrow. "Almost?"

"You can't be too careful," I murmur, going up on my toes and pressing a kiss against his lips.

I know that the party is celebrating Oakley and Justin, but I can't help but feel as if it's a celebration for all of us. My siblings are all starting to find their paths in life, and the bakery is going from strength to strength.

And the one thing there's no doubt this room is full of, it's love. And I know this is just the beginning of it all. There'll be plenty more to come in the future too.

EPILOGUE

CLOVER

I ENTER Cauldron Coffee Shop and gasp at the twinkling lights and perfectly placed decorations adorning the walls. It seems as if Willow and Azíl have raided the bakery's stash of Christmas decorations in order to pull this off, but done it in a way that makes it clear that they're not for the season.

A blown-up copy of my cookbook's cover sits on a board by the door, making this all suddenly feel very real.

Tyler squeezes my hand. "You okay?"

"I just can't believe that this is it," I murmur. "It's actually happening."

"Technically, it actually happens tomorrow," he points out. "Right now the only people who have seen your book are those who got advanced copies."

"I know, but it's still so surreal."

"Have you seen what people are saying?" he asks.

I shake my head. "I haven't dared to look."

"You should." He hands me his phone and I can see that he's gone to ObscureConnect and searched for the Broomstick Bakery hashtag. There are several posts and videos about the cookbook, and even a few of the advanced readers who have baked things from it already and posted photos of their creations.

Tears spring to my eyes as I read through what everyone is saying. "They like it?"

Tyler nods. "They seem to. The feedback so far is positive. You might have some people who question your use of emotions in cooking, but I think they'll be in the minority."

"That's to be expected, we have people who question that in the bakery itself too. I think it's a legitimate question. Do you think my author's note will be enough to counter that?" I ask.

"For most people."

The door to the flat upstairs opens and Willow appears, looking the perfect part of the host in a nice black dress that I know will allow her to easily make drinks without spilling on herself. "You're here already," she says.

I nod. "I let myself in."

"As you should. Azíl will be down in a minute, but I can get you drinks if you want. There's some champagne in the fridges for later, but the coffee machine is ready to go."

"You know what I'll have," I respond.

"Mmhmm, one pumpkin spice latte coming up. And for you, Tyler?"

"What do you recommend?" he asks.

I groan. "Don't get her started on that question."

Willow chuckles. "Give me a clue at least. I may be good at making drinks, but I'm not a mind reader."

"A cappuccino would be good."

"Want to add a magical shot?" She waves at the menu behind her.

"Courage," I mutter.

She takes me seriously and picks up a small bottle of it to add to my drink.

"Wait, do they actually work?" Tyler asks.

"They better, for what I pay for them," Willow

responds. "But yes, they work. They're not like the emotions at the bakery."

"I didn't realise that was a thing," Tyler says.

"Here, try this one." She sets a shot on the side. "It doesn't taste of anything, but you'll feel more alert. It's a little like caffeine I guess, but with more of a kick."

Tyler picks the shot off the counter and peels off the top. He knocks it back, his eyes widening as the effects hit his system. "Whoa, that's both cool and terrifying."

Willow chuckles. "I only stock things that can have a positive effect, but like anything, you shouldn't overdo it."

"I can tell why, that thing would give a kick."

My cousin's satisfied smile makes me laugh, even as she turns away to start making our drinks.

"Are we ready other than the drinks?" I ask.

Willow nods. "Azíl should be getting the cakes right about now, he's had a great time putting them all in the perfect position on the platters. You'd think he'd baked them himself."

"I'm surprised he hasn't tried."

"Oh he did. He attempted to make the tarte tatin from your book. I love him, but wow, baking is *not* a skill he possesses." Willow sets the drinks down on the side. "Oh, look, the others are here." She nods towards the door.

I turn to see my family arrive. Nerves spring to life inside me as they make their way into the coffee shop. It's strange to think that they're all here for the launch of my book, especially when it would never have happened without them. I hope they don't think it's weird that we're having the party here instead of at the bakery, but there really isn't enough room there for a gathering with this many people.

Tyler rubs my arm gently. "It's going to be fine," he reassures me.

"You can't possibly know that."

"Of course I do. I'm your editor, remember? I've seen how hard you've worked at this."

"But you're also biased."

"Maybe, but I wouldn't lie to you. Tonight is going to show you just how amazing you are. And your family, friends, and the cookbook world are all here because they want to see you succeed."

"You're sweet for saying that." Even if there's a part of me that doesn't believe it's true.

"I mean it. You're no longer just a baker, Clover, you're the person who brought this all to life. If you can't see how amazing you are, then think about how amazing the bakery is. And that all of these people are here to celebrate that and learn more about how you do it."

"You make it sound like I've given away all of our secrets."

His lips quirk up into a bemused smile. "I'm well aware that isn't true. Though I'm hoping I'll get to spend many years to come learning the rest of them."

"I hope to spend many years sharing them with you," I respond.

"Then let's go celebrate all things Clover and Broomstick Bakery," he says. "And I'm not just saying that because I spied some baklava on the platters with the cakes."

"Did you really think I wouldn't make some for tonight when I know it's your favourite?"

He leans in and kisses my cheek, drawing me into the room to talk to people and remind me that what he's saying is the truth.

Tonight is about the bakery, and the new chapter that's starting for us all. Even if it's scary to think about what's to come, I know that it's going to be fun to uncover it. And no matter what the future holds, I don't have to do it alone. I have my family, and I have Tyler.

What more could a witch need?

* * *

Thank you for reading *The Baklava Witch*, I hope you enjoyed it! While this is the end of the *Broomstick Bakery* series, you can find more of the Parkes siblings in the *Cauldron Coffee Shop* series, which follows Willow and Azíl: http:// books2read.com/pumpkinspiceandallthingsnice

You can also download a free Broomstick Bakery story featuring Ash and Ellie here: https://books. authorlauragreenwood.co.uk/1tpnl326xa

AUTHOR NOTE

Thank you for reading *The Baklava Witch,* I hope you enjoyed it.

It's hard to believe that the *Broomstick Bakery* series is over. When I first started it, I had no idea what the response would be like, and I've honestly been blown away by the support I've received for it. If I had more siblings to write about, or if I'd introduced more staff members at the bakery, then perhaps I would have continued the series further, but Oakley, Hazel, and Ash's stories were all completely written and finalised before I realised that it was going to resonate with as many people as it did. Rather than force the series to be something it was never planned to be, I decided to stick to the original plan of following the Parkes siblings.

However, if you want to see more of Clover and

the others, you still can! They appear as side characters in Willow and Azíl's series, *Cauldron Coffee Shop*. Clover in particular has a bigger role later in the series and pops up in most of the books from *Cinnamon Cocoa And Far To Go*.

Or, if you just want more witches in paranormal romance, you can hop over to my *Obscure Academy* series and *Potion Making For Disastrous Witches*, which follows Michaela, a witch who isn't very good at making potions, even though she tries to be!

I will have more sweet paranormal romance with characters not at an academy coming soon - make sure you're following me on social media for news about that!

Thank you so much for reading and supporting the *Broomstick Bakery* series, it genuinely means the world to me. I didn't think people would want my light-hearted sweet bakery paranormal romance when I started writing it, but I knew I'd have fun, so did it anyway. The fact that people have loved it as much as they have is really touching to me.

If you want to keep up to date with new releases and other news, you can join my Facebook Reader Group or mailing list.

Stay safe & happy reading!

- Laura

Signed Paperback & Merchandise:

You can find signed paperbacks, hardcovers, and merchandise based on my series (including stickers, magnets, face masks, and more!) via my website: https://www.authorlauragreenwood.co.uk/p/shop.html

Series List:

* denotes a completed series

The Obscure World

A paranormal & urban fantasy world where supernaturals live out in the open alongside humans. Each series can be read on its own, but there are cameos from past characters and mentions of previous events.

Cauldron Coffee Shop - Broomstick Bakery - Obscure Academy - The Shifter Season - Grimalkin Academy* - City Of Blood* - Grimalkin Vampires* - Supernatural Retrieval Agency* - Sabre Woods Academy* - Scythe Grove Academy*

* * *

The Forgotten Gods World

A fantasy romance world based on Egyptian mythology. Each series can be read on its own, but there are cameos from past characters and mentions of previous events.

Forgotten Gods

The Egyptian Empire

A modern fantasy world set in an alternative timeline where the Egyptian Empire never fell.

The Apprentice Of Anubis

The Paranormal Council Universe

A paranormal romance & urban fantasy world where paranormals are hidden away from the human world,

and are in search of their fated mates. Each series can be read on its own, but there are cameos from past characters and mentions of previous events.

The Paranormal Council Series* - Paranormal Criminal Investigations* - The Necromancer Council*

Other Series

Amethyst's Wand Shop Mysteries (with Arizona Tape) - Purple Oasis (with Arizona Tape) - Grimm Academy - Beyond The Curse* - The Vampire Detective* (with Arizona Tape) - The Dragon Duels* - Speed Dating With The Denizens Of The Underworld (shared world) - Seven Wardens* (with Skye MacKinnon) - Firehouse Witches* (with Lacey Carter Andersen & L.A. Boruff)

ABOUT LAURA GREENWOOD

Laura is a USA Today Bestselling Author of paranormal, fantasy, urban fantasy, and contemporary romance. When she's not writing, she drinks a lot of tea, tries to resist French macarons, and works towards a diploma in Egyptology. She lives in the UK, where most of her books are set. Laura specialises in quick reads, whether you're looking for a swoonworthy romance for the bath, or an action-packed adventure for your latest journey, you'll find the perfect match amongst her books!

Follow the Author

- Website: www.authorlauragreenwood.co.uk
- Mailing List: www.authorlauragreenwood.co.uk/p/mailing-list-sign-up.html
- Facebook Group: http://facebook.com/groups/theparanormalcouncil

- Facebook Page: http://facebook.com/authorlauragreenwood
- Bookbub: www.bookbub.com/authors/laura-greenwood